USBORNE COMPUTER GUID

101 THINGS TO DO ON THE INTERNET

Mark Wallace

Designed and illustrated by Isaac Quaye and Zöe Wray

Edited by Philippa Wingate

Cover by Isaac Quaye
Additional illustration by John Russell
Technical consultant: Nigel Williams, Director of Childnet International
Additional consultancy by Liam Devany
Managing editor: Jane Chisholm
Managing designer: Stephen Wright

In this book you'll find 101 projects which will help you to discover the fantastic variety of things you can do on the Internet. When you are connected to the Internet, or "online", you will have a huge range of information and resources available to you. Each project will show you something fun to do, or teach you a new skill to make using the Internet easier.

Use the projects as a starting point to explore what the Internet has to offer, and to find areas that you particularly like.

TACKLING THE PROJECTS

The projects in this book are divided into themes such as space, films and food, so that you can easily find information that interests you. You can tackle the projects in any order, dipping into the book wherever you like. Each project will give you all the information you need to complete it, or you will be directed to a page where you can find the relevant extra help.

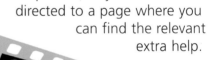

HOW DO I GET ONLINE?

To carry out the projects in this book, you will need a multimedia computer, a device called a modem, and a telephone line (see pages 6 and 7).

You will also need to be connected to the Internet. To do this, you'll need to pay a company called an Internet service provider (ISP). Some well-known service providers are *AOL*, *MSN* and *Prodigy*. You could ask friends who use the Internet which ISP they use. If you buy an Internet magazine such as *Wired*, *.net* or *Byte*, you will find advertisements for ISPs, detailing their services and giving telephone numbers to contact.

Call an ISP to ask about getting Internet access. Some companies have introductory offers, such as allowing you some time online for free.

Once you have selected an ISP, it will send you instructions about how to set up your equipment. It will provide you with the software you need to get connected to the Internet, and instructions about installing it on your computer.

If you have problems with your computer hardware or software, your ISP will have a helpline which you can call for advice.

USING THIS BOOK

Once you have an Internet connection, most of the projects in this book can be done using programs that you probably already have on your computer.

The instructions in this book are aimed at personal computer users with *Microsoft® Windows®95*. But it doesn't matter if you haven't got exactly the same programs as the ones described here. Most programs of the same type work in a similar way, although the commands may be slightly different. Projects that require an additional program include instructions about how to get hold of the relevant software.

Most of the images in this book were obtained from the World Wide Web. They look a bit blurry, like the images on a computer screen.

The Internet, or the Net, is a huge computer network linking together millions of smaller networks all over the world. A massive amount of information is stored on these computers. When you are connected to the Net, you gain access to this information. You can use it to find out about people and places, to buy things, to communicate with a variety of other people, and to make new friends.

The main areas of the Net that people use are the World Wide Web, e-mail, online chat and discussion groups.

CYBERSPACE

When you use the Net, you travel through imaginary space called cyberspace. When you visit different places and talk to people, you are moving in cyberspace.

THE WORLD WIDE WEB

The World Wide Web, also known as the Web or WWW, is made up of millions of documents called Web pages. These pages can include text, still and moving pictures, and sound.

Most organizations on the Web have sets of pages which are linked together. These sets of pages are called Web sites.

The Web is the fastest-growing part of the Internet, with hundreds of new pages appearing each day. You can use it to get up-to-date information about almost any subject.

Every Web page has its own address, called a URL (Uniform Resource Locator). This makes it easy to find pages and go back to pages you've visited before.

This is an imaginary URL:

http://www.usborne.com/home.htm

This tells you that the page is a Web page.

This tells you the name of the computer on which the page is kept.

This tells the computer the filename of the page.

This URL tells your computer that the page is called *home.html*, and that it is stored on a computer at *www.usborne.com*.

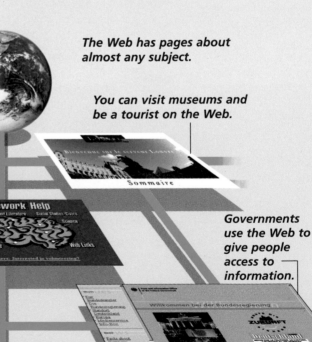

The Web has pages about almost any subject.

You can visit museums and be a tourist on the Web.

You can go shopping on the Web.

Lots of Web sites help people to do research work.

There are thousands of games on the Web.

Governments use the Web to give people access to information.

E-MAIL

Electronic mail, or e-mail, is a method of using your computer to send messages to other Net users. You can contact people, no matter where they are in the world, in a few minutes. It only costs the price of a local telephone call to send and receive messages.

ONLINE CHAT

Lots of people use the Net to chat online. You can type a message onto your screen which is then seen by other users. You can use your computer to talk on the telephone and even take part in a videoconference, where you talk to a person and see them at the same time.

The Net is creating a huge variety of new ways to communicate with other people.

DISCUSSION GROUPS

There are two kinds of discussion groups available on the Internet: newsgroups and mailing lists.

Newsgroups are Net discussion groups. They work like bulletin boards – users leave messages in a newsgroup which other people can read and respond to.

Many people discuss their interests using Net mailing lists. Mailing list members exchange ideas via e-mails.

Newsgroups and mailing lists deal with all sorts of interests, from science fiction to gymnastics. You can use them to find out more about an interest you have, find other people who share your interest, and leave messages for a whole group of people. There are over 25,000 newsgroups, and a similar number of mailing lists, on the Net.

To use the Internet, you must have a computer, a modem, and a telephone line. You normally have to pay an Internet service provider (see page 3) to get connected to the Net.

WHAT TYPE OF COMPUTER?

You don't have to have a high-powered computer to use the Net. You can connect to the Net as long as your PC has at least a 386 processor chip. If you have a Macintosh, it should have a 8036 chip, or better.

Computer memory and storage space is measured in megabytes (MB). Your computer needs at least 16MB of RAM (Random Access Memory) to use Internet and Web software.

Software, and information you want to keep permanently, is stored on your computer's hard disk. Your computer needs at least 200MB of free hard disk space to store Internet and Web software.

This diagram shows how a computer connects to the Internet.

WHAT IS A MODEM?

A modem is a device which enables computers to communicate with each other via telephone lines. A computer produces data in the form of pulses of electricity known as digital signals. A modem converts digital signals into waves that can travel along telephone lines. These waves are known as analog signals.

There are two types of modems that can be used with desktop computers: internal modems and external modems. An internal modem fits inside your computer. An external modem is connected to your computer by a cable which plugs into a socket at the back of your computer. This socket is called a serial port.

Modems transfer data to and from the Internet at different speeds. The speed is measured in bits per second (bps). It is a good idea to use a modem which works at a speed of at least 28,800 bps. The faster your modem works, the less time you will spend transferring information from the Net onto your computer.

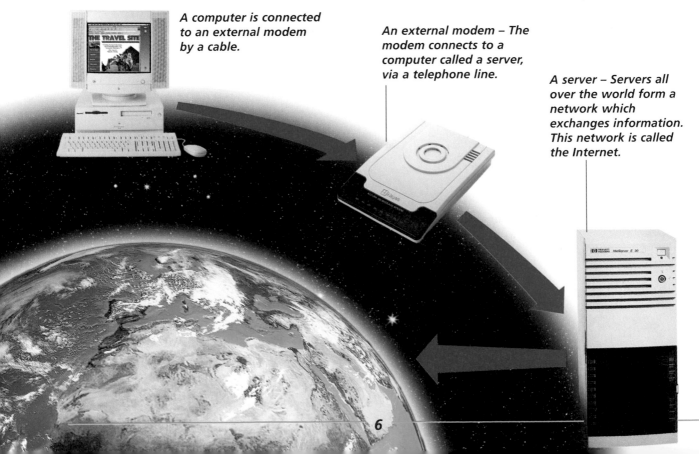

A computer is connected to an external modem by a cable.

An external modem – The modem connects to a computer called a server, via a telephone line.

A server – Servers all over the world form a network which exchanges information. This network is called the Internet.

EXTRA EQUIPMENT

For some of the projects in this book you'll need extra equipment.

These extra pieces of hardware all connect to your computer via cables.

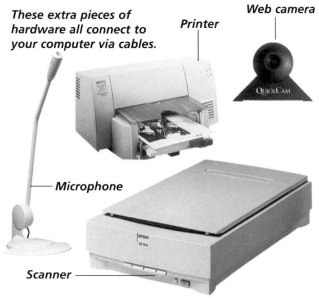

Web camera

Printer

Microphone

Scanner

 To print Web pages, pictures or text, you'll need a printer. Alternatively you could take a floppy disk containing documents to a printing and copying business that can print them for you.

 If you have a multimedia computer, it will probably be equipped with speakers and a sound card, so that you will be able to hear music or sounds via the Net. If you don't want to disturb other people around you, you could use headphones instead of speakers.

 To record sounds and save them on your computer you'll need to have a microphone. You can connect this to your computer.

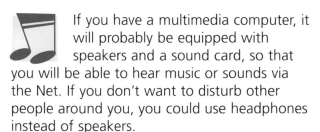 To convert pictures into files, so that you can view them on your computer or send them via the Net, you will need a machine called a scanner. There's more information about scanners in project 89.

 A Web camera is a type of video camera which can be linked to your computer. It records pictures which are broadcast directly onto your computer, and can be sent via the Net. Lots of Web sites show live pictures from Web cameras.

 Some games require a graphics card to show 3-D effects.

INTERNET SOFTWARE

When you arrange your Internet connection with a service provider, they will send you instructions on how to get the software you'll need. Most companies send the software on CD-ROM.

Internet software is regularly updated. You can update the software on your computer by downloading the latest versions of programs free of charge from the Web. You may also find software updates on the CDs that come with many Internet-related magazines.

BEFORE YOU START

As you do the projects in this book, you will create new files on your computer. It's a good idea to create a folder on your computer's hard disk or C drive, where you can keep all the documents you make using this book. This way you won't lose track of anything you've produced using the Net.

To create your own folder, click on *Start* and select *Programs*. Select *Windows Explorer*. You'll see a window showing the folders stored on your computer.

Go to the *File* menu and select *New*, then *Folder*. In the right-hand window you'll see a new folder with the title *New Folder* highlighted. Name your folder *Projects* by clicking on the title and typing in the name.

A browser is the program which you use to look at Web pages. You will probably have one included with your Internet software. The two most frequently used browsers are *Microsoft® Internet Explorer*, shown here, and *Netscape Navigator®*. They both work in a similar way.

The Microsoft Internet Explorer browser window

Use the Back button to see the last page you looked at.

Pages are displayed in this area.

Web page title **Use the Stop *button if you decide you no longer want to download a particular page.*** **Menu bar** **Address box**

1 GO TO A WEB PAGE

The easiest way to find a Web page is to type its address into your browser's address or location box. Connect up to the Net and start up your browser. Click in the address box and delete the URL if there is one showing. Type in the URL for the White House's Web site: **http://www.whitehouse.gov/**, and press *Enter*. Your browser will download the entry page of the White House's Web site. A site's entry page is called its home page.

This is the White House's home page.

2 SHORT CUT TO A WEB PAGE

When you find a Web page you like, you can create a short cut in your browser so you can find it again quickly. These short cuts are called "Bookmarks" in *Netscape Navigator*, and "Favorites" in *Microsoft Internet Explorer*. They are useful, because URLs are not easy to remember. It's a good idea to create a short cut whenever you find a page that you like. This makes it easier to remember sites and visit them again later.

To create a short cut in *Netscape Navigator*, download your chosen page, go to *Bookmarks* on your menu bar, and select *Add Bookmark*. To look at the Web page which you've bookmarked, simply click on its name from the *Bookmarks* menu while you are connected to the Internet.

To create a short cut in *Microsoft Internet Explorer*, download the page and select *Add to Favorites* from the *Favorites* menu. To view the Web page later, click on its name from the *Favorites* menu while you are online.

There are so many pages and sites on the Web that it's easy to be swamped with information.

The best way to find pages with specific information is by using a program called a search service. There are two types of search service. One looks for Web pages that contain particular words. This type of search service is called a search engine or index. The other kind, called a directory, breaks down Web sites into categories and lists sites in each one. This type is useful for more general searching.

Search services are compiled by teams of editors, or by computers which sift through, and categorize, Web sites. Because there is so much material being added to the Web all the time, no search engine can list every Web site. When you are looking for information on a particular subject, it's a good idea to use at least two services to ensure you get a selection of relevant pages. Some services tell you about new, interesting, or popular sites. Many services also have their own news and weather pages.

SEARCH SERVICE WEB SITES

Search engines
http://www.altavista.digital.com/ AltaVista™

http://www.webcrawler.com/ WEBCRAWLER Just what you're looking for!

Directories
http://www.hotbot.com/ HOTBOT

http://www.mckinley.com/ MAGELLAN INTERNET GUIDE

http://www.infoseek.com/ infoseek℠

http://www.excite.com/ eXcite

http://www.yahoo.com/ YAHOO!®

http://www.lycos.com/ LYCOS®

(3) CARRY OUT A KEY WORD SEARCH

One way to search is by using key words. A key word is a word which sums up the subject of a page, or which appears a number of times on it.

Open your browser, connect to the Internet, and type in the URL for Webcrawler, at **http://www.webcrawler.com/**. Webcrawler is a search engine. You will see a box where you can type in your key word. This is called a query box. Try typing the word **chimpanzee** into the query box. Click on the *Search* button.

The search engine will compile a list of Web pages which contain that key word. The results are presented as a list of links. At the top of the list you'll see the number of results. Click on a link to visit one of the Web pages.

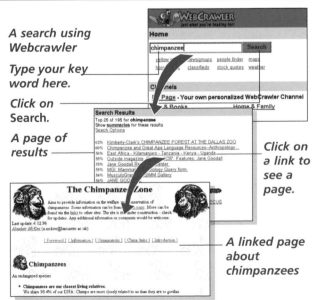

A search using Webcrawler

Type your key word here.

Click on Search.

A page of results

Click on a link to see a page.

A linked page about chimpanzees

4 SEARCH BY CATEGORY

When you search the Web using a directory, you gradually narrow down the subject area of the page you're looking for. You can do this using Yahoo! at **http://www.yahoo.com/**.

Say, for example, you want to see a page about a television cartoon. Start by clicking on *News & Media* on Yahoo!'s home page. A page of *News & Media* sub-categories will download. Select *Television*, and from the page which downloads, select *Shows*. On the next page, click on *Cartoons*. You will see a long list of titles of cartoons. Select one to view a list of Web pages devoted to that cartoon. Finally, choose a link and click on it to see the page.

Using the Yahoo! directory to find cartoon sites

5 PERSONALIZE A SEARCH ENGINE

Some search engines allow you to create a personalized page. This page will contain news about subjects that interest you, and you can add other information such as forthcoming birthdays and links to interesting sites.

You can create a personal page using Webcrawler (**http://www.webcrawler.com/**). From the home page, follow the link to *My Page*. You will see a sample of a personal page. Select *Personalize* and a form will download. Fill in this form, or click on *Form for non-US residents* if you live outside the USA. You will need to type in your town and region, your e-mail address, and a password. Click on *Submit Registration* when you've finished.

A second form will appear where you can specify the news and information you want to see on your personal page. You can select sections such as *Headline News*, *Entertainment News*, *Weather*, and *Movies*. Make your selections and click on *Submit Interests*.

Your personal page will appear. Click on the *Change* button next to any of the sections if you want to change the information which is shown on the page.

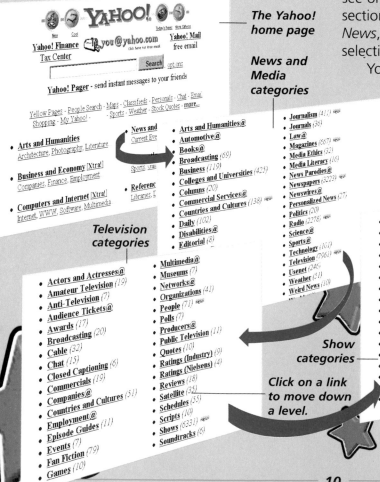

The Yahoo! home page

News and Media categories

Television categories

Show categories

Click on a link to move down a level.

As you move through the directory levels, the subject areas become more specialized.

6 DO AN ADVANCED SEARCH

Sometimes when you search using only one key word, it will produce thousands of results. If this happens, you can narrow down your search by doing an "advanced search". The best search engine for very detailed searches is AltaVista, at **http://www. altavista.digital.com/**.

A common method of performing an advanced search is to look for a specific name or phrase on a Web page. To do this you put quotation marks around the words. For example, to look for a Web page about a person called Maria Dixon you would type in **"Maria Dixon"**.

If you want to find a Web page featuring several words which don't necessarily appear together, put a **+** sign in front of each word. For example, you could find a page about the vaccinations you need if you are going to Indonesia by typing in **+vaccinations +Indonesia**.

You can use similar methods to exclude pages. So if you want to search for a Web page about travel vaccinations, but you don't want information about rabies, use the **-** sign, as in **+vaccinations -rabies**.

An advanced search using AltaVista

Type the search words in the box and click on the Search button.

A results page

Click on a link to see a Web page.

CHANGING WEB ADDRESSES

Because the Web is developing so quickly, it is common for URLs to change. You may find that URLs listed in this book have changed by the time you use them. If you find that a Web site has moved, use a search service to find it, or a similar site if it has been removed altogether. Search using the name of the site, or a suitable key word.

A list of cartoons

- Real Ghostbusters
- ReBoot@
- Ren and Stimpy *(8)*
- Road Rover *(4)*
- Robotech *(53)*
- Rocko's Modern Life *(12)*
- Rocky and Bullwinkle *(5)*
- Roland Rat - about Roland Rat and his friends Errol the Hams... Glenis the Guinea Pig and Little Reggie.
- Rugrats, The *(12)*
- Sam and Max - offici... ...e about the Fox cartoon.
- Samurai Pizza Cats *(...*
- Scooby Doo *(27)*
- She-Ra *(5)*
- Shirt Tales, The
- Simpsons, The *(443)* NEW!
- Sky Dancers - Queen Skyla and her academy students fight to s... from the threat of Vortex and its master Sky Clone.
- Smurfs, The *(19)*
- South Park *(124)* NEW!

The official Rugrats home page on the Nickelodeon site at http://www.nick.com/ and http://www.nickelodeon.co.uk/

E-mail is a great way to keep in touch with people and is one of the most popular features of the Internet. The projects here will help you use e-mail and find new people to exchange messages with.

Your service provider (see page 7) will probably have given you an e-mail program. The projects in this section use *Netscape Messenger*, which is provided with *Netscape Communicator*, but you will find that other e-mail programs work in a similar way.

(7) FIND AN E-PAL

Everyone who is connected to the Internet has an e-mail address. This identifies where their messages will be sent to. Here is an imaginary e-mail address:

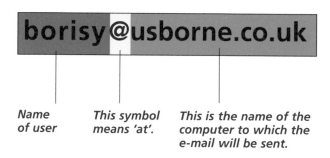

Name of user

This symbol means 'at'.

This is the name of the computer to which the e-mail will be sent.

If you don't know anyone who has an e-mail address, but you want to send someone a message, you need an e-pal. An e-pal is like a pen friend, but instead of writing letters to each other, you exchange e-mails.

One place to find an e-pal is at the Kids' Space Connection Web site at **http://www. KS-connection.com/**. From the home page, click on *Penpal Box*. You will see a list of letter-boxes for e-pals of different ages. Click on one of these to download a page containing a list of e-pals and their e-mail addresses. Each person on the list has written a short message about their interests. To send an e-mail to one of them, note down their address and follow the instructions in project 8. Make sure you read the site's guidelines about messages.

(8) SEND AN E-MAIL

E-mail is very quick and cheap to use, because it only costs the same as a local phone call to send messages. It usually takes only a few minutes for a message to reach its destination.

To send some mail, open your e-mail program. A window similar to the one shown below will appear.

The **Netscape Messenger** *window*

Click here to create a new e-mail.

Button bar

When you receive mail, the titles of messages will appear here.

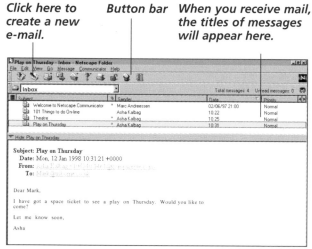

Click on the *New Message* button to create a new message. A window like the one below will appear. Click in the address box and type in the e-mail address of the person you're sending it to. Click in the main box and type your message. Think of a title for the e-mail and type it in the *Subject:* box. Go online and click on the *Send* button to send the message.

Netscape Messenger's Composition *window*

Click here to send the e-mail while you are online.

Type the address in here.

Give the message a title.

Type your message in here.

9 DESIGN AN E-MAIL SIGNATURE

Some e-mail programs let you make your messages more personal by adding a special signature to them. This could be a picture made from letters and numbers, or it could include a quotation or joke.

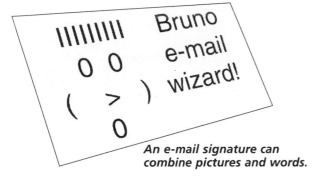

An e-mail signature can combine pictures and words.

You can use any word processing program to design a signature. Start a new document and type in the text you would like to use. Try to make it no more than four lines long, so that it doesn't take too long to download. Select *File*, then *Save*, and give the file a name.

Next, you need to instruct your e-mail program to attach the signature to all your messages. Open up your e-mail program. If you are using *Netscape Messenger*, select *Edit* then *Preferences*. The *Preferences* dialog box will open. Double-click on *Mail & Groups* and click on *Identity*. Select *Choose* to find your signature file, highlight it, and click *OK*. Your signature will be added to each e-mail you send.

10 SEND AN ANIMATED MESSAGE

You can send an animated e-mail message to someone using the Activegram site at **http://www.activegram.com/**. From the home page, click on *Sentiments*. You will see a list of categories including *Birthdays* and *Greetings*. Click on one of these to see a set of pictures. Select one to see it moving.

When you find an animated picture you like, scroll down the page and fill in the online form to send it to someone.

This animated message shows a dog eating a piece of toast.

If you know what type of computer and e-mail program you're sending the message to, fill in these details on the form. If not, click beside *Not Sure*. When the form is complete, click on *Email It Now!*. When the person receives the e-mail, the animated picture may appear automatically. If not, the e-mail will contain the URL of a Web page on which they can find the animation.

SAFETY

Be careful what information you give out in e-mails and in your e-mail signature. Don't include a signature containing your address or telephone number on e-mails you send to strangers. *Never* arrange to meet anyone you get to know over the Internet.

The Internet gives you access to a huge variety of programs that you can copy, or download, onto your computer. These two pages show you how.

Some programs can be added to your browser to enable it to show particular features of Web pages, such as video clips or interactive games. This type of program is known as a plug-in. If a Web page has been created using a plug-in which you don't have, you'll usually see a link to instructions on how to get it when you download the page.

SECURITY WARNINGS

Some Web pages require you to enter words onto them. For example, you often have to type in information before you download a program, or when you use search services. When you try to send information across the Internet in this way, your browser may display a window warning you that the information is not secure. This means it could be seen by somebody else. If you follow the safety guidelines throughout this book, it will be safe for you just to click *OK* in this window.

(11) DOWNLOAD A PLUG-IN

RealPlayer™ is a plug-in which enables you to listen to sound clips and watch video images via the Net. For example, you can use it to listen to most Web radio stations and hear sound clips on many music sites. You can download it from **http://www.real.com/ products/player/**.

From the home page, click on *RealPlayer*. You will see a form that asks for your name and information about your computer system. This will ensure that you download the most suitable version of the program for your computer. When you have completed the form, click on *Download FREE RealPlayer*.

Next you will see a page with links to sites around the world. Select the link to the site geographically nearest to where you are.

You will see a *File Download* window. Select *Save this program to disk* and click on *OK*. A *Save As* window will appear. Browse through the folders on your C drive and select the *Temp* folder as the save destination. This file should appear with the main ones on your C drive, like *System* and *Programs*.

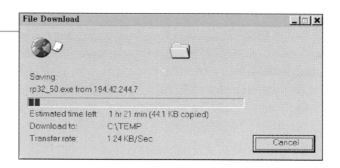

The File Download *window*

A new *File Download* window will appear. This tells you the name of the program file and gives you an estimate of how much time it will take to download. A *Download complete* window will appear when the program has been downloaded successfully. Use project 12 to install *RealPlayer* on your computer.

GETTING STUCK

There are lots of different ways of installing programs so the instructions on these pages may not work for every program that you download. You will usually find full installation instructions for a particular program on the Web site that features it, or in a *Help* or *Read Me* file that downloads at the same time as the program files.

(12) INSTALL A PLUG-IN

A program such as *RealPlayer* (see project 11) will normally automatically install itself on your computer if you carry out the following instructions. Make sure you are off-line and your browser is closed. Open *Windows Explorer* (to find it, click on *Start* and then *Programs*), and find the *Temp* folder where you saved *RealPlayer's* program file. Double-click on this to start up the installation process.

You will see a *Setup* screen. This gives you the instructions you'll need to install *RealPlayer*. Click on *Next* after you read each screen, and fill in any information, such as your name and e-mail address, when you are asked for it.

An *Installation* screen will appear. This will tell you where the *RealPlayer* program will be installed on your C drive. This is usually a folder called **C:\Program Files\Real\Player** or **C:\Real\Player**. Click *Next* to continue.

You will see a list of the browsers on your computer. (You'll probably only have one.) Place a mark in the box next to each browser listed and click *Next*. On the next screen, click *Next* and then *<Finish>*.

A *Progress* window will appear while *RealPlayer* is being installed on your computer. You'll see a window telling you when the installation process is complete.

(13) UNZIP A PROGRAM

Most programs you download will be in the form of "zip" files. These are files that have been compressed so that they take up less room when stored on a computer's hard disk. They can also be sent across the Net more quickly. Zip files have filenames ending in *.zip*.

One place where you will come across zip files is the GamesDomain site at **http://www.gamesdomain.com/**. This has lots of games which you can download. When you find a game you would like to try out, use the method described in project 11 to download its file.

Before you can use a program that has been zipped, you need to decompress or unzip it. To do this, you will need a program called *WinZip* if you use a PC, or *Stuffit* if you use a Mac. You can download *WinZip* from **http://www.winzip.com/** and *Stuffit* from **http://www.aladdinsys.com/**.

The following instructions explain how to unzip a zip file with *WinZip 6.3*. Open *WinZip*. You'll see a license agreement. To continue using the program, click *I Agree*. The *WinZip Wizard* window shown here may appear on screen. (If it does not, select *Wizard...* from the *File* menu in the window that does appear.)

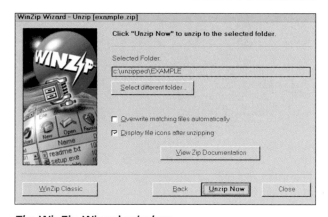

The **WinZip Wizard** *window*

Winzip Wizard will guide you through the process of unzipping the program and installing it on your computer. During this process, you'll see a list of zip files stored on your computer. You'll need to select the name of the zipped game file you downloaded. *Winzip Wizard* will tell you where it will store the program on your computer when it has finished. It usually unzips programs into a folder called **C:\Unzipped**.

When you want to play the game, use *Windows Explorer* to find this folder and look for a filename ending in *.exe*. Double-click on this filename to start the game.

Your travels on the Internet
need not be confined to the
planet Earth. From the safety of your
computer, you can explore deep space,
visit Mars, look at far-flung galaxies, and
ask astronauts all about their lives.

(14) VISIT THE SURFACE OF MARS

There are thousands of fascinating
pictures of the planets in our galaxy on the
Web. NASA's Web site contains a large range of
pictures from space. NASA is the USA's space
agency. It runs all of America's space missions,
and controls the information which comes back
from them.

To see pictures of Mars, start up your
browser and connect to the Net. Type in the
URL for NASA: **http://www.nasa.gov/**. Your
computer will download NASA's home page.

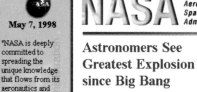

NASA's home page

Scroll down the page, and click on the link
to *Multimedia Gallery*. From the menu which
appears, select *Photo Gallery*. You will see a list
of different subject areas. Click on one of these
to see a page with a set of small pictures. Click
on one to see a larger version of the image.

You can find pictures of the surface of Mars
by clicking on *Space Science* on the NASA
home page, then *Missions*, and *Mars
Pathfinder*. You will see a page with
information and pictures.

To make sure you see the most recent
photographs available, you can use a search
engine to find material which has only just
been added to the Web. AltaVista's Advanced
Search feature at **http://www.altavista.
digital.com/** allows you to search the Web by
date. Type in a key word (see project 3), in this
case **Mars**, in the main box. To find Web sites
about Mars updated within the last month,
type in the date one month ago in the *From:*
box. Type today's date in the *To:* box. Click on
Search for a list of Web sites.

**These pictures of Mars first appeared on Nasa's
Web site in 1997.**

15 LOOK AT PICTURES FROM SPACE

The Hubble space telescope has been transmitting pictures from Earth's orbit since 1993. You can look at some of these pictures on the NASA Web site (**http://www.nasa.gov/**). Click on the *Multimedia Gallery* link, and then the *Photo Gallery* link. Scroll down to *Astronomy*, and use the *Space Telescope Science Institute/Hubble Space Telescope Public Release Images* link to see a menu of pictures.

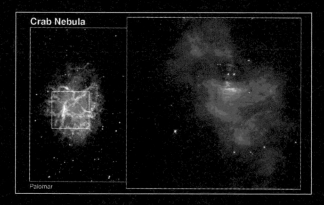

Hubble pictures from NASA's Web site

The picture menu is made up of a set of small pictures known as thumbnails. When you click on one, the computer downloads a larger version of the image. Web sites with lots of graphics, like NASA's, often use thumbnails to save people from spending a long time downloading images they don't want to see.

You can find out more about Hubble on NASA's Starchild site at **http://starchild.gsfc.nasa.gov/**.

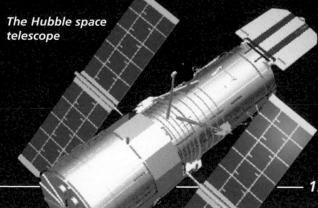

The Hubble space telescope

16 CONTACT AN ASTRONAUT

Have you ever wondered exactly what it is like to live in space? Now you can ask astronauts about their food, or how they sleep when they're weightless, by sending questions to them using an online form.

The Ask An Astronaut home page at http://www.nss.org/askastro

There are several Web sites which let you contact astronauts. The National Space Society Ask An Astronaut Web site at **http://www.nss.org/askastro/** contains interviews with different astronauts on a regular basis. You can submit your questions, and after a few weeks the astronaut will answer some of the questions which people have asked. The answers appear on the Web site.

On the Ask An Astronaut home page, click on the hyperlink to *Submit Your Question!*. A form will appear for you to fill in your name and e-mail address. Many Web sites use online forms like this. Information is sent via the Internet like an e-mail, but using the Web instead of a separate e-mail program. When you have filled in the form, click on *Submit Question*.

Don't forget to check back on the Web page to see whether an astronaut has answered your question.

There's a wealth of information about the natural world on the Net. You can get advice on looking after your pet, and contact organizations who provide information about different types of animals and plants, and how to protect them.

(17) GET HELP WITH YOUR PET

Whatever pet you have, there's bound to be helpful information about its breed, and how best to care for it, on the Web. A good place to search for this is Acmepet, at **http://www.acmepet.com/**. This Web site, like many others, has a built-in search facility, which

works like a search engine. From the home page, search the site by typing the breed of your pet into the *Search* box and clicking on *Search*. You'll see a list of links to relevant articles.

Pictures of animals in their natural habitats taken from the Web

(18) SEND A PICTURE WITH AN E-MAIL

You can use the Internet to send and receive pictures. One of the easiest ways to do this is by attaching them to e-mail messages.

One place to find amazing photographs is the American Museum of Natural History's endangered species Web site. This site contains information about rare animals, such as cheetahs and rhinoceroses. It's at **http://www.amnh. org/Exhibition/ Expedition/Endangered**. It is important to type this URL with the capital letters shown here.

Ann's Photo Gallery at http://www. inmind.com/people/amartin/ has pictures of wolves like this one.

When you have found a picture to send, click on it with your right mouse button. Select *Save Image As* (or something similar) from the menu which appears. In the next dialog box, select the *Projects* folder you created on page 7. The picture will already have a filename, so you can simply click on *OK* to save it.

To attach the picture to an e-mail, open your e-mail program. Create a new e-mail (see project 8), and compose your message. Click on *Attachment*. Select *Attach File* from the new window. In the next window, browse to find the name of your saved picture file. Select it, and click on *OK*. When you are ready, connect up to the Net, and send the message in the usual way.

19 PRINT A PICTURE FROM THE WEB

You can print out pictures you find on the Web to use in projects. Say, for example, you wanted to print out a picture of a parrot. To find a picture, you could try the Online Book of Parrots at **http://www.ub.tu-clausthal.de/ 2p_welcome.html**.

Save your chosen picture using the method described in project 18. In the *Save as type* drop-down list, select *Bitmap*, add *.bmp* to the filename, and click on *Save*. Now disconnect from the Net. You don't need to be online while you print out your picture.

Before you can print out your picture, you need to open it in a graphics program such as *Paint*. To do this, start up *Paint* then select *Paste From* on the *Edit* menu. A window will appear. Browse to find the picture file, and click on *OK*. Your picture will appear on screen. Select *Print* from the *File* menu to print it out.

You may want to make changes to a picture before you print it out. For example, you could add some words to turn it into a poster. You can use *Paint* to do this.

You can print any of the pictures you find on the Web. This picture shows two macaws with bright plumage.

20 SIGN AN ONLINE PETITION

Many Web sites allow you to get involved with campaigns and make your voice heard by signing online petitions. One of the largest wildlife organizations is the World Wide Fund For Nature (**http://www.panda.org/**). It has Web sites in a lot of countries and often uses online petitions to press for changes.

A selection of the conservation sites available on the Web

National Wildlife Foundation at http://www. nwf.org/

Treasured Earth Network at http://www. ten.org/

WWF-UK at http://www.wwf-uk.org/

The online petitions produced by organizations such as conservation groups normally consist of a statement or request with an online form attached. To add your name to the petition, fill in details, such as your name and e-mail address, on the form. Then click on a *Send* link. The organization creating the petition will deliver it to the government or person at which it is aimed. The more names that are on it, the more likely it is to be noticed.

The Web is a rich source of information for fans of all kinds of sports. You can use the Net to find out latest scores, get news about a team, or find out about future sporting events.

22 FIND SPORTS STARS

Many famous sportsmen and women have more than one Web site devoted to them. They are likely to have an official site, set up with their permission and cooperation and a number of "unofficial" Web sites, usually created by their fans.

You could try finding an official site about the tennis player Pete Sampras using a search engine. Type in his name, plus the word **official** as your key words (see project 3). To find a selection of unofficial sites, simply omit the word "official".

The official site about Olympique Lyonnais, a French soccer team

21 PREVIEW A FUTURE EVENT

The Web is a useful resource for finding out about events that haven't happened yet. For example, the next Olympics will be held in Sydney, Australia, in the year 2000, but you can already visit its Web site at **http://www. sydney.olympic.org/**.

To get some information about the sports at the 2000 Olympics, click on the logo to go to the home page, and click on *Sports*. You will see a list of the sports which will be included in the Games. Click on one of these, for example *Gymnastics*, to see a page with more information about that sport.

The logo for the Sydney 2000 Olympics

23 GET THE LATEST SCORE

News agencies and broadcasting companies often maintain Web pages which are constantly updated with sporting information and results. One very thorough online sports service is CNN/Sports Illustrated at **http://www.cnnsi.com/**.

Explore the site to find information about a sport that interests you. To ensure that the information on a page you are looking at is completely up-to-date, you should click on your browser's *Reload* button from time to time. This will instruct your browser to download the latest version of the Web page, which should contain the current scores or results.

㉔ FIND A SPORTS MAILING LIST

You can exchange messages about sports with other enthusiasts by joining a mailing list. This is a discussion group which sends e-mails to people interested in a particular subject. Some mailing lists deal with individual teams, others cover whole sports.

To help you find the name and e-mail address of a mailing list about a particular subject, there is a search engine called Liszt at **http://www.liszt.com/**. The Liszt Web site includes links to Web pages with instructions on how to subscribe to, and use, particular mailing lists.

Find mailing lists using the Liszt home page.

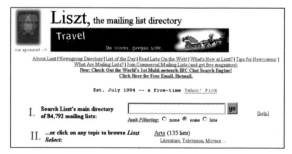

㉕ JOIN A SPORTS MAILING LIST

Joining a mailing list is as easy as sending an e-mail. Some lists have their own Web sites which tell you exactly what to do. You normally have to send an e-mail with the word *subscribe* in the title to a particular address. You can find the e-mail address for a mailing list using Liszt, as in project 24.

When you join a mailing list, you will normally be sent an e-mail with all the essential information about the list. This will include how to send your own e-mails to everyone on the list, and how to unsubscribe from the list.

The London-based soccer club Chelsea has a Web site at http://www. chelseafc.co.uk/.

Like most soccer teams, Chelsea soccer club has a mailing list. Its e-mail address is chelsea@cogs.susx.ac.uk

MAILING LIST TIPS

• You should expect to wait a day or two for a response to any messages you send to a mailing list.
• Create a separate folder in your e-mail program to hold your mailing list e-mails.
• Follow the mailing list's guidelines about the kind of messages you can send in.
• Unsubscribe if you are going on holiday, and resubscribe when you get home, or you may end up with hundreds of e-mails.

It's possible to listen to radio broadcasts and recordings over the Net, as well as making your own music online. You can also join a newsgroup (see page 5) to debate with other Net users who share your interests.

(26) JOIN A MUSIC NEWSGROUP

To join a newsgroup that discusses the kind of music you enjoy, you will need a program called a newsreader. Most browsers include a newsreader. The instructions in this book are for *Netscape Collabra*, which is part of *Netscape Communicator*. (In this program newsgroups are called discussion groups.)

The first time you use newsgroups, you need to download a list of the ones available. To do this, start up your newsreader and go online. From the main screen, click on the *Subscribe* button. The *Subscribe to Discussion Groups* window will appear, and it will download a list of newsgroups. This can take several minutes.

Netscape Collabra's Subscribe to Discussion Groups *window*

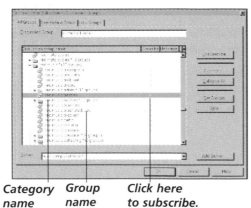

Category name   *Group name*   *Click here to subscribe.*

When the list has downloaded, you'll see a list of categories, for example **rec** and **sci**. Each one contains several newsgroups. The name of a category describes the type of newsgroups it contains. For example, **sci** contains newsgroups in which science is discussed. Categories are shown as folders and newsgroups are represented by a speech bubble icon.

Click on the **+** sign next to a category folder to see a list of the newsgroups it contains. Most newsgroups about music are in the **alt** (alternative) and **rec** (recreational activities) categories. When you see the title of a newsgroup you'd like to join, such as the one shown below, click in the *Subscribe* column next to its title. Click *OK* to return to the main news screen.

A newsgroup title

rec.music.beatles

Category name   *The rest of the title indicates what the newsgroup is about.*

To read the messages in a newsgroup, you need to know the name of your news server. This is the computer that gives you access to newsgroups. You can find out what it is called by asking your service provider (see page 3). On the main news screen, click on the **+** symbol next to the name of your news server to see a list of all the newsgroups to which you have subscribed. Double-click on the name of one of them to download the titles of its messages, known as postings. Highlight a title to read a posting.

The Netscape Collabra *window*

Tool bar   *Menu of newsgroups*   *Titles of postings to rec.music. beatles*   *The text of a posting appears here.*

NEWSGROUP TIPS

• Look out for a message called Frequently Asked Questions or FAQ. This is a list of the questions most often asked by new members. Read this before you start sending messages to a newsgroup.

• If people send messages you don't like, leave the newsgroup.

• Never give out personal information such as your surname, address, or telephone number.

27 DISCUSS MUSIC VIA THE NET

You can give your opinion on a song by sending a message to the newsgroup you found in project 26. Sending a message to a newsgroup is called posting. Before you do this, read the other postings to the newsgroup over a few days. This is called lurking. It's a good idea to lurk so you don't post an inappropriate message.

To post a message, click on *To News* on your newsreader's toolbar. A window will appear in which you can type your message.

28 LISTEN TO WEB RADIO

Many radio stations have Web sites where you can listen to broadcasts online. You will need to download a plug-in to hear them. This is usually *RealPlayer*. (See project 11 for information on downloading this plug-in.)

Once you have downloaded *RealPlayer*, go to a Web radio site. You will find Britain's Virgin Radio at **http://www.virginradio.co.uk/**. Follow the *click here* link on its home page. On the page which appears, click on *RealPlayer 3.0*. The *RealPlayer* window will open, and you will hear the station through headphones or speakers attached to your computer.

29 MAKE MUSIC ON THE WEB

You can create your own music, and work with other musicians, using a program called *DRGN* (the Distributed Real-time Groove Network). You can download this from the Net for free.

To download *DRGN*, visit the Res Rocket site at **http://www.resrocket. com/**. Select *Getting Started* to get basic information about using the program. Click on *Software & Support*, then *Download DRGN* to start downloading it. On the next screen, select *download via WWW*. Use the instructions in projects 11 and 12 to download and install it. Click on the *Next* button on the page while it's downloading. Fill in the form which appears to select a password to use with the program.

DRGN comes with complete instructions. Read these carefully. You can use *DRGN* to create music tracks using the keys on a computer keyboard. You select the instrument you want to sound like, and select the notes you want to play. You can then join other musicians in an area called a *DRGN* studio. Together, you can combine different tracks to create a song. Musicians call this a "jamming" session.

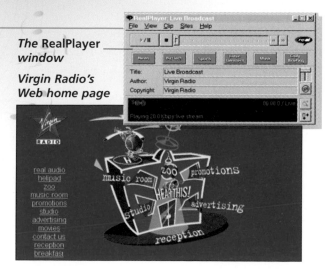

*The **RealPlayer** window*

Virgin Radio's Web home page

There are lots of ways to use the Internet to help you do research, write essays, or get assistance with your homework. You may want to find some extra facts or a good picture to add to your work. If you do find a Web site useful, don't forget to mention its name and address in your work to show that you've used it.

Sites designed to help with your homework

(30) ASK EXPERTS FOR HELP

There are many sites on the Web where you can get help from experts on a range of subjects, from science to art.

The Homework Help site at **http://www.startribune.com/homework/**, for example, invites you to send in questions and get a personal reply from a teacher.

Imagine, for example, you needed to find the answer to the question "Which insect species has the longest life cycle?" On the home page, click on the *Science* link. First you should check that the question hasn't already been asked. To do this, click on *search engine*. A search page will appear. Type in the word **insects** and click on *Search*. You will see a page showing a list of people who've asked questions about insects. Click on a name to read that person's question and the answer.

Once you are sure that nobody else has already asked your question, return to the main *Science* page and click on the *Zoology* link.

On the next page, click on *Animals*. You will see a list of relevant questions and answers.

To ask your question, scroll down to the online form at the bottom of the page. Click on the name box and type in your first name. Next, click on the question box and type in your question. Press *Post My Message* to send your question to the site. The question will be posted onto the Web page. The Homework Help site tries to answer questions within 24 hours. Check back later to see if an answer has been posted.

Don't forget that when you contact teachers for help they need time to respond. If they're in another country, there may be a time difference of several hours. So don't expect a reply immediately.

A page showing questions and answers

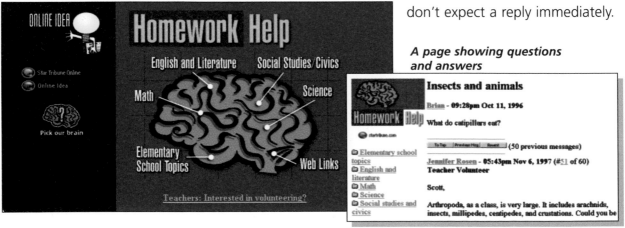

31 LISTEN TO OTHER LANGUAGES

You can learn some foreign words or phrases by listening to them being spoken on Web pages. One site where you can do this is the Foreign Languages For Travelers site, at **http://www.travlang.com/languages/**. This site has pages covering 60 languages.

Say, for example, you want to listen to someone saying hello in Mandarin, the official language in China. From the home page, select *English* from the drop-down menu and click on the link to *Mandarin*. You will see a page of categories, including *Basic Words*, *Numbers*, and *Travel*. *Basic Words* should already be selected. Click on the *Submit* button to download a page containing a list of basic words. This list includes the Mandarin for hello, *Ni hao*. Click on the words to hear them being spoken.

Choose a language from this page.

Click on a word or phrase to hear it being pronounced.

32 USE WEB REFERENCE TOOLS

There is a large selection of reference tools, such as encyclopedias and dictionaries, on the Web. Once you get used to using them, you will be able to look up information quickly and easily.

A particularly useful site is the Research It! site at **http://www.itools.com/research-it/**. One of the things you can do on this site is find out about famous people. To do this, scroll down the home page to the *Biographical* section, which is listed under *Library Tools* and *People*. Type in the name of a person, for example the composer Mozart, and click on *look it up!* A page will download showing information about Mozart's life.

Other reference tools on the Research It! site include an online dictionary, a thesaurus and a rhyme finder.

A biography found using Research It!

The Research It! Web site includes several different reference tools.

There is a vast selection of computer games for Net users to sample and play. There are games you can download onto your computer and play by yourself, or you can join in online games with players all over the world.

(33) DOWNLOAD A NEW GAME

A good site for finding games is GamesDomain's Web site at **http://www. gamesdomain.com/**. You will find both free games and games that you can buy. Many of the games that are for sale have free demonstration versions which you can download and try out before you decide to buy.

To find a game, click on *Downloads* on the home page. On the next page, click on the link to programs that will suit the operating system you have installed on your computer. For example, if you have *Windows 95*, select *Win 95*. A menu of different types of games will appear. Select *Newest 100* to see a list of new games. Click on one, and you will see more details about the game, and a list of sites from which you can download it. Select the nearest site to where you live, and the game will start to download.

Use projects 11 and 13 to help you download and install the game.

(34) PLAY CHESS ONLINE

The Yahoo! Games site at **http://play. yahoo.com/** has a variety of different games that you can play online with other players. Select a game that you want to play from the home page, for example *Chess*. The first time you use

Yahoo! Games, you need to register by completing an online form. To do this, click on *Get Registered* and follow the instructions.

Once you have registered, a menu will appear showing the different levels of chess you can play at, and the number of people currently playing in each level. Click on the level you want and you'll see a list of current games. Look for a game that only has one player and click on *Join* to play against them. When you see a window containing a game board, you can start the game.

You can also play Backgammon, Checkers, Cribbage and other games on the Yahoo! Games site.

Here are some of the games you will find on the Web. **Virtual Pool 2**

Sim City 2000 Network Edition

Monopoly

35 JOIN AN ONLINE ADVENTURE

You can enter a whole new world with role-playing games. Some of these games, such as *Magic: The Gathering*, can be played online. To use *Magic: The Gathering*, you will have to buy the program on CD-ROM. Visit its Web site at **http://www.gathering.net/**. If you decide to buy it, you can order the program from the MicroProse Online Store site, at **http://store.advaccess.com/ microprose/**. To play the game online, you will also need a program called *ManaLink*, which you can download from the Net for free. (See project 49 for help with ordering items online, and page 45 for security information.)

An image from the Magic: The Gathering Web site

Magic: The Gathering is based on a card game. Each player has a set of cards, which represent magic spells and can be used in the game. Players travel around a vast fantasy world, meeting characters who are playing the game at the same time. Playing the game online can take up a lot of time, which can be expensive. You can also play the game on your own off-line, going on quests and adventures.

Screen shots from Magic: The Gathering

A character in the game

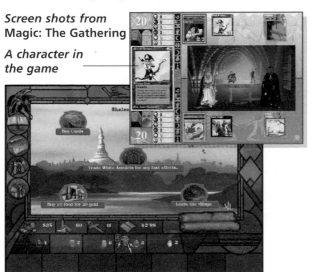

36 RACE CARS ON THE NET

There are games in which you can race cars against other competitors on the Net. Some of these games use amazing 3-D graphics to make it look like you're really in the driving seat.

Ultimate Race Pro is a 3-D race game. You can download a free demonstration version of the game from its Web site at **http://www. ultimaterace.com/**. From this page, follow the link to *Download*. Use projects 11 and 13 to download and install the demo. You may need to have an extra graphics card installed on your computer to play the game (see page 7).

The demonstration version of *Ultimate Race Pro* only allows you to play the game on your own. To play it online against other Net users, you'll need to buy the full version of the game on CD-ROM and set up an account to use it. You can order it from the MicroProse Online Store at **http://store.advaccess.com/ microprose/**.

Scenes from games of Ultimate Race Pro

Movie buffs everywhere love the Internet, because it has a wealth of information about new and current films. There are hundreds of Web sites about movie stars set up by their fans. The Net is also a great source of gossip and news about films which are currently in production or about to be released.

(37) FIND FILMS IN YOUR AREA

You can use the Web to plan a trip to see a film. One site you may find useful is the Internet Movie Database. It contains a set of links to sites which show which films are showing in many different countries.

Visit the Web site at **http://us.imdb.com/Cinemas/**. Click on your country from the list which appears to see links to listings for your area. Simply click on the relevant link to find information about films on locally.

A selection of movie-related Web sites

Men In Black at http://www.meninblack.com/

Space Jam at http://www.spacejam.com/

Courtesy Warner Bros. Online

(38) MAKE YOUR OWN MOVIE ONLINE

The Interactive Simulation site at **http://library.advanced.org/10015/data/interact/sim/** lets you create an imaginary film and then tells you how it might have done at the box office.

To start creating a movie, click on *New Simulation* and follow the instructions on screen. You will have to select a password so that the site can save your simulation as you go along. This means you can stop working on it at any time, then return to it later.

Creating a movie involves making a lot of decisions. For example, you will be required to select an ending for the film and decide which shots to use when you are filming. There will always be several options you can choose from. Be careful to keep within your film's budget.

When you complete the film, the Web site will produce a page with a summary of how successful your imaginary film was.

This Web page asks you to choose a camera angle for your movie.

Some shots are more expensive to film than others.

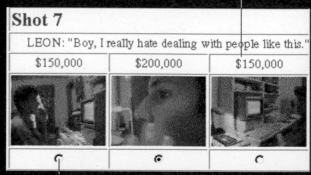

Click in a circle to select a shot.

(39) SUBMIT A REVIEW

Why not tell other people about a film you've enjoyed watching by sending a review to a Web site? One site devoted to movie news and reviews is Popcorn at **http://www. hotpopcorn.com/**. This has a section where you can submit your own comments about films you've seen.

To submit a review, or any other comments, follow the link to *Email Sky!*, and fill in the online form on the page which appears. Check back at a later date to see whether your comments have been added to the *Readback the Feedback* page.

The Warner Brothers movie and TV site at http://www.warnerbros.com/

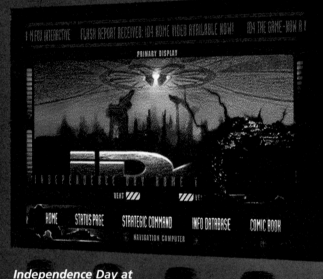

Courtesy Warner Bros. Online

Independence Day at http://www.id4movie.com/

(40) WATCH A FILM PREVIEW

Most new film releases have their own Web sites. On some sites you can watch previews. Occasionally you can see a preview on the Web before it is shown elsewhere.

Start by finding a film's official Web site using the Internet Movie Database (IMDb) at **http://www.imdb.com/**. To find a Web site using IMDb, click on *SEARCH* on the home page. On the page which appears, type in the title of the film and click on *search*. Select the film you want from the list which appears. Click on the *Official* icon (shown here) and scroll down the page to find a link to the official site.

IMDb's Official icon

When you have downloaded a film's Web site, you may see a link on which you must click to watch a preview. The page that appears will display instructions about how to see the preview. Since previews are video clips, you will need a plug-in to view them (see pages 14-15).

The preview will be shown in a box in your browser window, or in a new window. You'll hear the soundtrack through your speakers or headphones.

Previews can take a long time to download, so be certain that you want to watch the one you've chosen before you begin to download it.

The Internet is used to exchange and publish data gathered by computers all over the world. So whether you want to study the annual rainfall in Australia or tomorrow's forecast for France, you'll find Web sites with detailed weather maps and information.

41 PRINT OUT A WEATHER MAP

You can print out a map showing the weather for a country or a continent. One place to find weather maps is Yahoo! Weather, at **http://weather.yahoo.com/**. From its home page, click on the link to *Weather Maps*. Find your region on the grid, and click on *Outlook*. You will see a map showing the latest forecast.

You can print out any Web page exactly as you see it on screen, including all the words and pictures. To do this, select *Print* from the *File* menu while the page is displayed in your browser window. If you have to pay for the amount of time you spend connected to the Internet, it is a good idea to go off-line before you print out Web pages.

A weather map from Yahoo! Weather

42 CHECK THE WEATHER ON THIS DAY IN HISTORY

Can you remember what the weather was like on this day last year? Probably not; but you can find sites that have records of this information on the Web. The NCDC Climate Visualization Web site at **http://www.ncdc. noaa.gov/onlineprod/drought/xmgr.html** has a collection of maps covering the United States of America that show weather information for any day, right back to 1893.

You can see up to four maps at once, each showing different information. From the home page, click on *Contour/Vectors*. Select the number of maps you want to see from the pull-down menu, and click on *Next*. On the next page, select a date for the first map. In the *Parameter* section, you can select daily maximum or minimum temperatures, rainfall, or snowfall. Scroll down and select the region you want to display.

When you have selected the information for all the maps, click on *Next*. You will see a confirmation screen. This tells you which maps you've selected. Check it and click on *Submit*.

The BBC Weather Centre at **http://www. bbc.co.uk/weather/** also has information about the weather on this day in history. To see this, click on *The Almanac* on the home page.

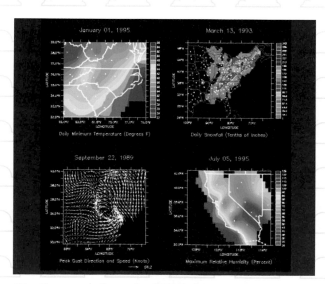

Weather maps from the NCDC site

43 USE YOUR OWN WEATHER PROGRAM

To see up-to-date information about the weather all over the world on your computer's desktop, you can get a program called *WinWeather* from the Web.

The *WinWeather* program displaying weather data

City	Date	Temp	Hum.	Press.	Wind	Wthr	Fct
London	N/A	N/A	N/A	N/A	N/A	N/A	N/A
New York	20 Jan 1998 09:51 AM EST	+35°	69%	29.98	9 WNW		
San Francisco	N/A	N/A	N/A	N/A	N/A	N/A	N/A
Los Angeles	N/A	N/A	N/A	N/A	N/A	N/A	N/A
San Francisco	20 Jan 1998 06:56 AM PST	+46°	89%	30.03	0 NORTH	scattered clouds	
Los Angeles	20 Jan 1998 06:50 AM PST	+51°	71%	29.93	4		
London	1PM JAN 20 1998	+41°	N/A	N/A	N/A		N/A

Temperature —————

This symbol indicates that the weather is cloudy.

To download a free 30-day trial version of *WinWeather*, visit the Insanely Great Software Web site at **http://www.igsnet.com/**. Follow the *WinWeather* link from the home page to download the program. (See projects 11 and 13 for help with downloading and installing it.)

When you start *WinWeather* and go online, you will see a window showing the weather in different cities. The program will take a few minutes to collect current information. You can change the choice of cities by going to the *Configure* menu and selecting *Configure Cities*. A menu of cities to choose from will appear.

WinWeather also features direct access to weather Web cameras (see project 85). To see live weather pictures, select *International Cams* from the *Images* menu, and choose a camera to look through.

44 JOIN A WEATHER PROJECT

You can get involved in a project studying and comparing the weather with Net users in other countries on the One Sky, Many Voices site at **http://onesky.engin.umich. edu/**. Click on the name of one of the projects to find out all about it.

To register for a project, click on *REGISTER* on the home page, and fill in the online form which appears. Click on *Submit* and you will be sent an e-mail containing full instructions.

One Sky, Many Voices organizes weather-based projects for students all over the world.

You can find lots of weather pictures like these on the Australian Severe Weather site at http://australian severeweather. simplenet.com/

Dinosaurs may be extinct on Earth, but they're still thriving on the Internet. Many museums have online dinosaur exhibitions where you can learn about prehistoric life. Other sites enable you to test your knowledge. There are plenty of dinosaur pictures to look at on the Web and you can even watch dinosaurs coming back to life on your screen.

(45) VISIT A DINOSAUR MUSEUM

One way to learn about dinosaurs is by touring an online museum, such as the Hunterian Museum. The museum's entrance hall is at **http://www.gla.ac.uk/Museum/ tour/entrance/**.

Take an online tour at the Hunterian Museum.

From the entrance hall, use the direction buttons to explore the museum. To see a plan of the museum, click on *Map*. You can go directly to any of the rooms by clicking on the appropriate part of the map. Once you are in an exhibition room, you can click on some of the exhibits to find out more about them.

(46) EXPLORE A FILM WEB SITE

Many Web sites have behind-the-scenes information about how films are made. For example, you'll find out fascinating facts about how the special effects in the dinosaur movie *The Lost World* were achieved by visiting its Web site at **http://www.lost-world.com/**. To access the main site, click on the picture on the Web page which appears. From the Web page showing an office, you can explore the site by clicking on the map which is shown hanging on a wall.

Follow the link to *Site B* to get technical secrets from the film. The Web site is split into several areas, each one with different information. Try clicking on *Hunter's Camp* to see how the dinosaurs were animated, and how scenes were filmed.

Dinosaur pictures from Dinosauria at http://www.dinosauria.com/

47 DOWNLOAD A DINOSAUR SCREEN SAVER

The Web offers a vast selection of animated screen savers which you can install on your computer. To find a screen saver with dinosaurs on it, search the Web using **+dinosaur +"screen saver"** (see project 6). A list of links will appear. Follow a link to find information about a dinosaur screen saver.

Click on a screen saver's link to download it. In the window which appears, select your browser's *Download* folder as the destination of your screen saver. Unzip your screen saver using the instructions given in project 13, and place it in your *Windows/System* folder.

To activate the screen saver, go offline and click on your *Start* button. Select *Settings* and *Control Panel*. Double-click on the *Display* icon. Select the *Screen Saver* tab from the *Display Properties* window. Click on the *Screen Saver* pull-down menu to see a list of your system's screen savers. There are normally several to choose from.

Click on the name of the dinosaur screen saver, and then click *OK* to activate it. You can set the exact length of time for the computer to wait before it displays the screen saver in the *Wait* box.

The screen saver pull-down menu

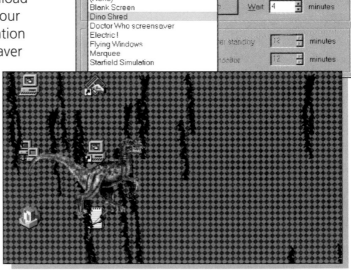

This screen saver is of a dinosaur which appears to tear up the desktop.

48 DO A DINOSAUR QUIZ

Test your dinosaur knowledge by doing a quiz on the Web. The Question Mark site has a good one at **http://www.questionmark. com/qmwebquestions/dino2.htm**.

This page contains a list of questions with multiple choice answers. To select an answer to a question, click in the circle next to your choice. You may have to answer some questions by typing an answer into a box. When you've finished, click on the button at the bottom of the screen to find out the correct answers. You will also see your answers, and your score.

The Web gives you access to all kinds of pieces of writing, from poems to academic articles, and novels to teen magazines. You can read texts online or place an order for a paper version.

There are Web sites where you can have your own work published and on-going writing projects to join in.

49 SHOP AT AN INTERNET BOOKSTORE

Internet bookstores are Web sites which sell books. Their main advantage is that they can offer millions of titles, far more than you'll find in any store. They also feature articles about new books and authors, comments from readers, and recommendations.

One Internet bookstore is Amazon.com, at **http://www.amazon.com/**. To look at the books available to buy, use the search facility on its home page, or click on *Browse Subjects*. The site also has information on new books.

At Amazon.com, like many Internet shopping sites, you can use a device known as a shopping cart in which you gather all the books you want to buy. To place a book in the cart, click on the *Add it to your Shopping Cart* button.

To pay for the books you have chosen, you have to complete an online form. You will need to give the address where you want the books delivered and state how you are going to pay for them. Most people who buy things via the Web pay for their goods with a credit card. (To buy things online you need to be over 18. If you're not, ask someone who is to help you.) To find more information about shopping on the Net see pages 44-45.

A selection of Internet bookstores

http://www.amazon.com/

http://www.okukbooks.com/

http://www.barnesandnoble.com/

50 GET A POEM PUBLISHED ONLINE

Writers all over the world have had their stories and poems published on the Web.

One site that encourages Net users to submit work for publication is Positively Poetry at **http://advicom.net/~e-media/kv/poetry1.html**. To send your own poem, follow the *Submit* link from the home page and enter your poem onto the online form.

Alternatively, you can send in your poem by e-mail. Make sure you read the site's rules for submitting poems. One such rule is that the poem must not be over 25 lines in length. The site organizers choose poems to go on the site, and remove old ones after three months. The site always contains lots of poems to read.

51 ADD TO A NEVERENDING STORY

Some of the stories you'll find on the Web have been written jointly by a large number of people. They are called neverending stories. A neverending story starts when someone publishes the beginning of a story on a Web site and invites other people to send in contributions to continue the plot. These sections are put straight onto the Web, so that Net users can follow the story as it develops.

A good place to read a neverending story is the Kidpub site at **http://www.kidpub.org/kidpub/**. It has a different story each week. Click on the title of the neverending story on the home page to read this week's story.

To add to the story, click on the link at the bottom of the page and complete the online form that appears. You'll receive an e-mail explaining how to contribute. Anything you submit will be added to the story immediately.

Kidpub's home page

52 FIND A BOOK ONLINE

Many famous works of literature are published on the Net. The Internet Public Library at **http://www.ipl.org/** has links to over 5,000 books which are stored on Internet computers.

To help you find a particular play, poem or novel, this site includes a search engine. Say, for

The Internet Public Library home page

example, you want to find one of Shakespeare's sonnets. Click on *Online Texts* on the Internet Public Library home page. You will see a search page. Type **Shakespeare Sonnets** into the box and click on *Search*. You'll see a list of links to online versions of a book called *The Sonnets*.

Click on one of these links to download the book. This may take a few minutes. Then scroll down the page to find the sonnet you want to read. You could also print out the page (see project 41).

The Internet is fast becoming one of the most popular places to find the latest news. Search services and newspapers have Web sites on which stories appear almost as they happen.

53 GET THE LATEST NEWS

You can make sure that up-to-date news is sent to your computer automatically. To do this you will need a browser which uses "Push" channels. A Push channel is a window within your browser which, while you are online, continually gathers specific information for you, such as news stories or TV schedules.

Netscape Communicator 4, *Microsoft Internet Explorer 4*, or a later version of either browser, can include Push channels. *Netscape Communicator's* Push channel program is called *Netcaster* (find out more at **http://www. netscape.com/**). *Microsoft Internet Explorer* uses a program called *Webcaster* (see **http:// www.microsoft.com/**).

To start up *Netcaster*, select its name in *Netscape's* <u>C</u>ommunicator menu. To use *Webcaster*, click on *Internet Explorer's Channels* button. Your browser will guide you through the process of setting up a channel so you can get up-to-date information while you're online.

Newspaper Web sites from all over the world

http://www. lemonde.fr/

http://www. usatoday.com/

http://www.press.co.nz/

The BBC Online Push channel in Internet Explorer

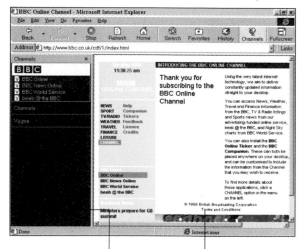

List of available channels   **BBC Online channel**

54 WRITE FOR A MAGAZINE

Why not contribute to a Web magazine that is created by people all over the world? Kidlink, at **http://www.kidlink.org/KIDPROJ/ Magazine/**, organizes a Web magazine. The articles it contains are written by young people from many different countries.

To take part in the magazine project yourself, you need to join its mailing list (see project 25). Send an e-mail to **listserv@listserv. nodak.edu** with the message *subscribe KIDPROJ* and your name. You will be sent more information about the magazine and the kind of articles you can write for it.

Kidlink's home page

(55) CREATE AN ONLINE NEWSPAPER

You can select the information you want to read by creating your own online newspaper. Crayon's Web site at **http://www. crayon.net/** creates your own set of links to news sites. You can use it each day to get the type of news that interests you.

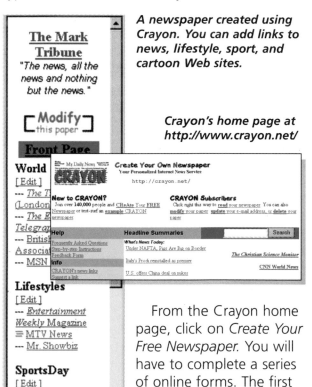

A newspaper created using Crayon. You can add links to news, lifestyle, sport, and cartoon Web sites.

Crayon's home page at http://www.crayon.net/

From the Crayon home page, click on *Create Your Free Newspaper*. You will have to complete a series of online forms. The first form asks you to enter your e-mail address and choose a password. The other forms ask you to choose exactly what you want your newspaper to look like and which news sites you want it to link to. For example, you can choose a title, motto and layout for your newspaper.

When you have finished, click on *Publish My Newspaper*. You will be shown the URL of the Web page on which your newspaper will appear. As your newspaper is personal, its URL includes your e-mail address so that other people cannot read it or find it by accident. The URL will be quite long so it's a good idea to create a short cut to it (see project 2).

(56) WORK WITH THE NEWS

You may find a news story on the Web which is relevant to a piece of work you're doing. It's easy to copy text from a Web page into a word processing program and insert it into an essay or project. First save all the text on the Web page by selecting *Save As* from the *File* menu. In the *Save as type* box, select *Plain text*, and change the ending of the file name from *.html* to *.txt*. Click on *OK* to save the file.

Go offline, close your browser, and open a word processing program. Select *File* and *Open*, and browse to find the document you saved. You will see the text from the Web page. You can change how the text looks and you can copy a section of text to use as a quote by highlighting it and using the *Copy* and *Paste* commands in your word processing program's *Edit* menu.

If you copy text from a Web site in this way, ensure that you make it clear that it is not your own work. You should also state where you found the information.

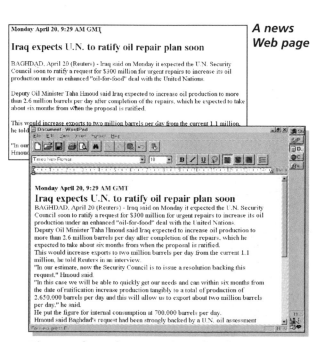

A news Web page

The text from the page above has been copied into a word processing program.

The Internet gives you access to millions of recipes for dishes from all over the world. There is also plenty of information about healthy eating. Many companies use the Net to publicize food products, and you can sometimes buy meals online.

You can find out how to make these dishes at http://www.ilovepasta.org/

57 FIND A RECIPE ON THE WEB

You can find the recipe for a specific dish by searching the Web using the names of its main ingredients. This is also a good way to find out what you could make with any ingredients you already have at home.

Gourmet World's site has information about food and cooking.

For example, a search using the words **+recipe +chicken +mushrooms** would give you a list of recipes including chicken and mushroom pie, and chicken casserole.

Gourmet World, at **http://www.gourmet world.com/**, has links to a wide range of recipes, information about restaurants, links to online food shops, and food facts. To find a recipe, click on *Culinary Center* on the home page, and select *Gourmet World Cookbook* from the page which appears. Next, select a category of food, such as *Casseroles*. A list of links to recipes will appear. Click on a link to see a recipe. If it sounds appetizing, you can print it out (see project 41) so that you can make it yourself.

58 ORDER FOOD ONLINE

To order a meal online, you have to find a local restaurant which offers an online order service. You place your order by filling in an online form. The food is delivered to your home when it is ready.

You could search by key word (see project 3) to find sites which offer this service. Use the type of food you want, the word **online**, and the name of your town, as key words. A search using **+pizza +online +London**, for example, will produce a list of results showing pizza restaurants in London which take online orders.

Pizza Online at http://www.pizzaonline.com/ has links to restaurants in the USA and Canada which accept online orders.

59 CREATE A VIRTUAL PIZZA

Imagine a pizza with sinks, footballs, and smiling faces as toppings. It may not sound very appetizing, but there is a Web site where you can create a virtual pizza with all kinds of strange ingredients. The Internet Pizza Server is at **http://www.ecst.csuchico.edu/~pizza/**.

To design a pizza, scroll down the home page, and click on the link to *Order and view a pizza over the Web*. You will see an online form that lists a variety of ingredients. To select a topping, place a mark in the box next to it. You could be conventional and choose olives, ground beef and green peppers. Alternatively, you could choose more unusual ingredients, such as beetles, road signs and kittens. You can create a truly bizarre combination on your virtual pizza.

When you've finished, click on *order pizza* to download your pizza. A page containing a picture of the pizza will appear on your screen.

This virtual pizza has beetles, nails, olives, salami and road signs on top.

60 GET RECIPES BY E-MAIL

You can get a regular supply of recipes by joining a mailing list (see project 25). Mm-recipes runs a list which sends out recipes, and lets its members respond to requests for recipes from other people. You will normally receive between 10 and 20 messages from the list each day, including recipes and cooking advice. To join, send an e-mail to **majordomo @idiscover.net** with the message *subscribe mm-recipes* (see project 8). You will be sent an e-mail containing instructions on how to use the mailing list.

61 PUT YOUR RECIPE ON THE WEB

Some Web sites encourage you to contribute your own recipes, which are then put on the site. CyberRecipes, at **http://www. cyberpages.com/recipe**, has a large collection of recipes arranged by the country they're from.

To add a recipe to the site, follow the link to *Please add your own recipe!* Fill in the online form, including your country, the title of the recipe, the ingredients, and the preparation instructions, and click on *Add This!*

Your recipe will be added to the Web site. You can see it by following the link from the home page to the initial letter of your country, and scrolling down the page to your recipe.

If you put a recipe on the Web, make sure that it's worded carefully, so that people can follow it successfully.

The Net is invaluable if you are planning a trip. You can use it to book tickets and get tourist information. There are thousands of Web sites which will tell you about countries, and suggest places to visit and things to see.

Alternatively, you can make a "virtual" journey, visiting sites across the world and even sending postcards without actually leaving your computer.

A Swiss travel gallery Web site

A gallery of travel pictures from China

The Jamaican Tourist Board Web site at http://www.jamaicatravel.com/

63 GET AN AIRLINE TIMETABLE

You can find timetables for planes and trains all over the world on the Web. One company which has online timetables is Air France, which operates flights all over the world. You can find a timetable at **http://www.airfrance.com/**.

To see a timetable, click on *Schedules* on the home page. A page will download with an online form. Fill in the departure city, destination, and date of travel, and click on *Submit*. A page showing a timetable of flights will appear.

62 FIND TRAVEL PICTURES

To get ideas for amazing places to visit, you can look at other people's travel pictures on the Web. Use a search service that specializes in locating images, such as Image Surfer at **http://isurf.yahoo.com/**.

To find travel pictures, follow the link to *Recreation* from the Image Surfer home page. On the next page, scroll down to *Travel*, and select a location, such as *Hawaii*. You will see a set of thumbnail pictures. These are linked to Web pages which may have more pictures.

64 FIND TOURIST INFORMATION

You can use the Web to get information about tourism in almost any country. One good way to find a range of information about travel to a country is to use Excite Travel at **http://city.net/**.

Say, for example, you wanted to find some information about Jamaica. From Excite Travel's home page, click on *Caribbean* on the map. A page with a map of the Caribbean will download. Click on *Jamaica* to see a list of links to sites relating to tourism there.

65 SEND AN E-MAIL POSTCARD

Use the Net to find postcards which you can e-mail to friends. The E-Cards Web site at **http://www.e-cards.com/** has a wide selection of designs to choose from.

To send a postcard, go to the home page and click on *Write & Send*. You'll see a list of the different categories into which the postcards are divided. For postcards of places, click on *Region Selector*. A page showing a world map will download. Click on the part of the world you want your card to show.

The next page contains a set of thumbnail images of the postcards you could send. Click on one to select it.

The card will appear on your screen with an online form. Write a message and fill in the recipient's e-mail address, and your own. When you've finished, click on the link to *Build & Preview this card!*.

When you send a postcard, it's not delivered directly to the recipient's e-mail address, but is stored at its own Web address. The recipient will be sent an e-mail saying that there is a postcard waiting at that address. The e-mail will also contain instructions on how to look at the card.

This e-card shows a picture from Indonesia.

The E-Cards world map

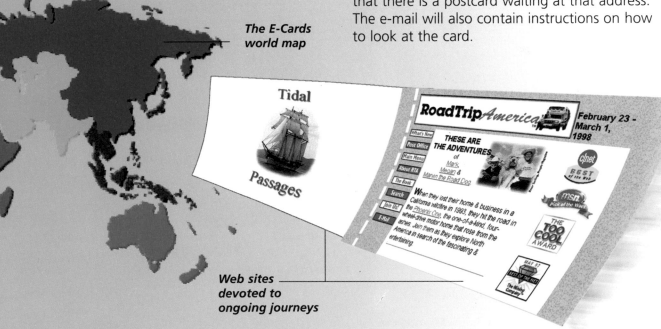

Web sites devoted to ongoing journeys

66 FOLLOW A WEB JOURNEY

Some people set up Web sites so they can report their journeys as they make them. You can see where they've been, and find out what their travel plans are. Sometimes the sites are updated every day. Their creators use laptop computers and connect to the Web by satellite phone to do this. Sites can be created from ships, cars or even planes.

One such site is the Road Trip America Web site, at **http://www.RoadTripAmerica.com/ index.html**. You can follow the adventures of a family which is driving around the USA in a mobile home. From the home page, see the latest bulletin from the family by clicking on *What's New*. You will see a page about the places they've visited recently.

The Net makes it possible to chat to other people who are online. You can make new friends across the world, or keep in contact with people you already know who are a long way away. Some Net users make arrangements to be online at specific times, so that people can find them and chat to them regularly.

67 USE AN INTERNET PHONE

You can use the Net to talk to people, just like using a telephone. To do this you will need some Internet telephone software, speakers and a microphone you can connect your computer. When you have installed the software, you can talk to people in other countries without having to pay long-distance call charges. You only have to pay for a local telephone call to your Internet access provider.

Find out about using an Internet phone on the VocalTec site at **http://www.vocaltec.com/**. This site also has software which you can download to start using a Net phone (see project 11).

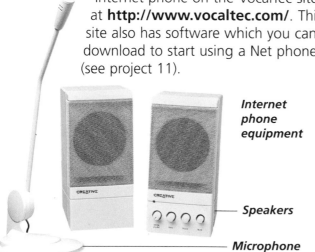

Internet phone equipment

Speakers

Microphone

SAFE CHATTING

• Don't continue talking to people who say things that you don't like.
• Be aware that people can pretend to be whoever they like when they chat online.
• Don't spend too much time chatting, as time spent online costs money.

68 CHAT TO PEOPLE OVER THE NET

One of the most well-established forms of online chat is Internet Relay Chat, or IRC. You need an IRC program to take part in this. With IRC, people chat to each other in groups called channels. Each channel has a title which covers the main interest of the group, such as *Teen* for teenage users.

A chat session in a program called **mIRC**

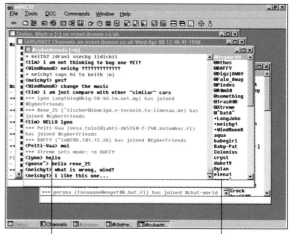

This window shows an ongoing chat.

List of people chatting

During a chat session you will see text written by other users appearing on your screen. To say something yourself, simply type it in and press *Return*. It will appear on your screen, and on the screens of all the other users, immediately. Other people can respond and start up conversations with you.

There are a number of IRC programs available free for a trial period. You can download one called *mIRC* from **http://www. mirc.co.uk/**. For help with downloading programs, see project 11. The mIRC Web site contains full instructions on how to install the program on your computer. You'll find more information in the *Help* files provided with *mIRC*. IRC is quite complicated to use, so you may want to print out the information in the *Help* files.

69 VISIT A VIRTUAL WORLD

On the Net you will find sites which contain amazing 3-D environments. These places, called virtual worlds, are created with Virtual Reality (VR). VR is the use of computers to create objects and places which appear to be real.

There are several types of virtual worlds which you can visit, including dungeons, landscapes and palaces. In some virtual worlds, known as 3-D chat rooms, you can chat to other people who are visiting that particular world at the same time as you.

To use a virtual world, you'll need to download a program from the Net.

Avatars talking in **Active Worlds**

A chat session using a program called **Active Worlds**

You can download a trial version of a VR program called *Onlive! Traveler* for free from **http://www.onlive.com/prod/trav/**. See project 11 for help with downloading programs.

Before you enter a virtual world, you have to choose an "avatar". This is a character which will represent you in the virtual world. It may look like a person, an animal or an alien. You use your arrow keys or your mouse to instruct your avatar to move.

When you come across avatars representing other people, you can start chatting. In some virtual worlds, you use your keyboard to type in what you want to say to the people you meet. In others, you can actually hear what people are saying and talk to them using a microphone.

A VR landscape from an online world called **Utopia**

70 HAVE A VIDEOCONFERENCE

A videoconference is a telephone conversation where you can see the person you're talking to.

You can use the Internet to have a videoconference. To do this, you will need a microphone, some speakers and a type of camera that you can attach to your computer, such as the Intel Internet Video Phone.

You will also need some software. The most popular program is *CU-SeeMe*. You can download a free version of this from the *CU-SeeMe* site at **http://cu-seeme.cornell.edu/**.

When you go online and make a call, you will see the person you're talking to in a window on your screen, and hear them speak through your speakers. The person you are contacting will need to have the same hardware and software as you.

The **CU-SeeMe** *Web site*

A video phone conversation

You can go shopping for almost anything using the Internet. Whether you want to buy clothes, gifts, or CDs, you'll find a wide range available through the Web. Many stores operate solely on the Web; they don't have any other branches. Others use the Web to promote or advertize their products and services.

71 VISIT A SHOPPING MALL

An online shopping mall is a site which brings together several Web shopping sites. You can access lots of stores from one site, just as you can at a real shopping mall.

The Internet Mall, for example, at **http://www.shopnow.com/**, has links to over 25,000 stores. You can use the search facility on the home page to find what you are looking for. Type a keyword into the box, select the section you want to search, and click on the *Search* button to download a list of links to shops. For example, to find stores selling cameras, search using the word **camera** in *The Technology Center*. Projects 49 and 72 explain how to pay for things online.

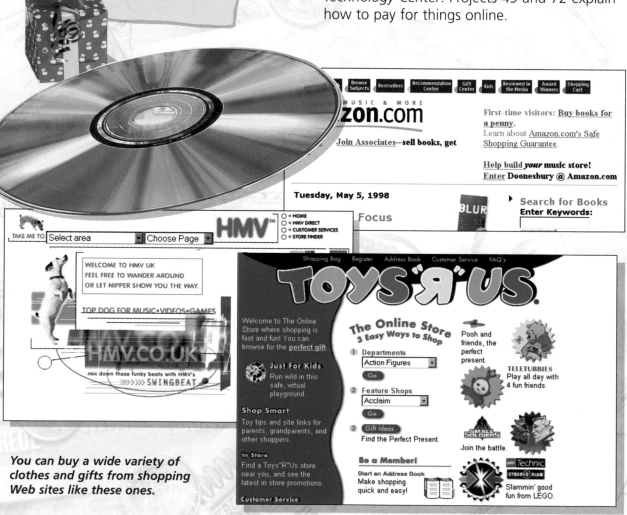

You can buy a wide variety of clothes and gifts from shopping Web sites like these ones.

72 USE ONLINE CASH

Some people pay for things that they buy on the Net with online cash. This is also called electronic cash, or eCash™. It has the same value as ordinary paper or metal money, but is actually data stored on a computer. The data can be used as money when it is transferred from one computer to another.

To use eCash, you have to withdraw it from your bank account using the Internet, and store it on your computer's hard disk. Search the Web for your bank's Web site and visit it to find out if your bank offers an eCash service. If it does, its site will have full instructions on how to set up the facility on your computer.

You can find out more about using eCash at the Digicash®Web site, at **http://www. digicash.com/**.

You can pay for things using an eCash™ purse, when the system is set up on your machine.

73 GUESS A WEB ADDRESS

Many companies have Web sites from which you can buy their products directly. If you don't already know the URL of a company's Web site, you can often guess it. Try typing in the company's name and adding *www.* before it and *.com* after it. For example you will find Nike at **http://www.nike.com/**.

© 1998 Mattel

Try to guess the URLs for the Barbie Web site and the Reebok Web site.

SECURITY

When you pay for things online, make sure the site you use is using a "secure" server. This means that information sent to the site, including addresses and credit card details, cannot be seen by anyone else. The information is turned into a code when it is sent across the Net, and changed back when it is received.

If you visit a secure server, your browser will display an unbroken key symbol, or a locked padlock. This usually appears in the bottom left corner of the browser window.

SHOPPING TIPS

• Always check whether an item you are buying can be delivered to the country you live in, as this is not always possible.
• Make sure the item you buy is exactly what you want, and that you can return it if you change your mind.
• To buy things online you need to be over 18. If you're not, ask an adult to help you.
• Some companies like to send e-mails to customers to give them news about their sites. There is usually a box on a company's order form you can place a mark in if you don't want to receive these e-mails.

The Internet brings together people from all over the world. This makes it a great place to learn about world environmental issues and to discover what you can do to help.

74 CHECK THE SMOG LEVEL IN L.A.

Cities throughout the world are falling victim to air pollution caused by traffic and factories. Los Angeles, California, is notorious for this kind of pollution, known as smog. Organizations there have pioneered the measurement and forecasting of air pollution.

You can check the current smog level in

 L.A. by visiting the Air Quality Management District page at **http:// www.aqmd.gov/**. Click on the lung icon to see today's smog readings, and the forecast for tomorrow.

75 EXPLORE A GREEN CITY

A good Web site for information about how to live a greener life is Recycle City's site, at **http://www.epa.gov/recyclecity/**. The site contains an imaginary environmentally-friendly city. Each part of the city has information about a different aspect of green living so you can learn as you explore.

From the home page, click on *Go to Recycle City!* to see the map shown here.

76 SEE A PANORAMIC SCENE

You can look around a natural scene using the *Quicktime* plug-in. Download and install it from **http://www.apple.com/ quicktime/** using projects 11, 12 and 13.

One place you can find a panoramic nature scene (a scene you can move around in and look at different views) is at **http://www. research.digital.com/PA/maps/parks-content.html**. Click on *Gallery* and choose a view from the page which appears. Wait for the picture to appear, and drag your cursor across it to look left or right.

A panoramic nature scene

You can explore the city by clicking on the map. For example, if you click on the bottom right corner, you'll see a close-up of that part of town. Click on a building, such as the factory, to see inside. You'll discover objects you can click on, such as a pile of paper in the factory, to discover how the city has been made greener.

A map of Recycle City

Visit the garage to discover how cars can be greener.

Visit this house to find out how to make your own home greener.

Groups all over the world have Web sites devoted to the environment. Some international organizations and companies maintain central sites which link to local sites in different countries. One example is the Greenpeace site. You'll find it at **http://www.greenpeace.org/**.

Greenpeace International

Greenpeace UK

Use the central Greenpeace site to find one of the national branches of the organization. On the home page, click on the link to *National Offices*. You will see a page with a set of flags which link to the different branches. Choose a country and click on its flag to visit the local Greenpeace site. On some countries' sites you can join Greenpeace online.

Use the links page to visit different branches.

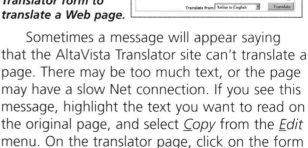

©Gunnberg/W3Comunication - http://w3.com.ar

Greenpeace Argentina

If any of the sites you want to visit are in other languages, you can use the AltaVista Translator site at **http://babelfish.altavista.digital.com/** to translate them.

Say, for example, you want to translate the Greenpeace Italy site at **http://www.greenpeace.it/** into English. On the AltaVista Translator home page, click on the form and type in Greenpeace Italy's URL. Select the languages you want to translate from and to, *Italian to English*, using the drop-down list. Finally, click on the *Translate* button. A translated version of the page will download.

Use the AltaVista Translator form to translate a Web page.

Sometimes a message will appear saying that the AltaVista Translator site can't translate a page. There may be too much text, or the page may have a slow Net connection. If you see this message, highlight the text you want to read on the original page, and select *Copy* from the *Edit* menu. On the translator page, click on the form and select *Paste* from the *Edit* menu. Select the languages and press *Translate*. You should see a translation of the text you highlighted.

You may never have seen a ghost or a UFO, but you'll find plenty of people on the Net who claim that they have. You can judge for yourself whether pictures of the yeti or the Loch Ness Monster posted on the Web are genuine. You can also find people who claim that they have been abducted by aliens or haunted by poltergeists. Almost every strange theory about the paranormal has its own Web site, and every bizarre sighting or investigation is thoroughly reported and discussed.

79 REPORT A UFO SIGHTING

Anyone who thinks they may have spotted an unidentified flying object (UFO) can report their sighting directly to professional investigators via the Net. Many UFO research organizations have sites on the Web. For example, the International Society For UFO Research (ISUR) has a Web site at **http://www. isur.com/**.

On this site you will find an archive of past UFO sightings and an online form which people can use to report the details of a new sighting. To see this online form, click on *Report a Sighting* on the home page. To explore the archive, follow the *UFO Archive* link.

A picture of a UFO from ISUR's Web site

80 EXPLAIN CROP CIRCLES

Crop circles are strange mathematical shapes which have appeared mysteriously in fields all over the world. Although some have been proved to be hoaxes, scientists remain baffled about many others.

You can find some of the different explanations for crop circles on the Web. A good source of information on all kinds of unexplained phenomena is the Fortean Times site at **http:/www.forteantimes.com/**. This is an "e-zine" (an electronic version of a printed magazine). It contains articles from the printed version, as well as extra features.

To read an article, go to the home page and select *articles*, and then *full article index*. A list of articles will download. Click on an article to read it.

The Fortean Times site has articles about crop circles.

Crop circle pictures posted on the Web

81 SEE A GHOST?

You can visit a Web site which is on the lookout for ghosts. The GhostWatcher, at **http://www.flyvision.org/sitelite/Houston/GhostWatcher/**, is run by a woman named June Houston, who believes her house is haunted. She has placed Web cameras (see project 85) throughout her house, so that visitors to the site can report anything suspicious to her.

To look around the house, go to the Ghostwatcher home page. Click on a location where cameras have been set up, for example there are a collection of cameras in June's basement. Select a camera to look through, and your browser will download an up-to-date picture of that area. If you do see anything unusual, fill in the online form under the picture and click on *Send your Report.*

The GhostWatcher home page

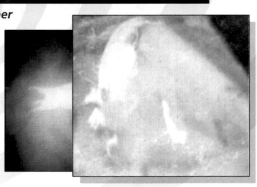

These pictures, from the Ghost Web site at http://www. ghostweb.com/, allegedly show genuine ghosts.

82 DOWNLOAD AN ALIEN CURSOR

Get aliens to invade your desktop by replacing your mouse pointers with moving pictures known as animated cursors. A lot of Web sites have animated cursors which you can download. To use animated cursors, you need *Windows 95.*

There is a good selection of alien cursors at **http://www.parkave.net/users/fitz/**. Download and unzip a few using projects 11 and 13. Put them into your *Cursors* folder, which is in the *Windows* directory on your C drive.

To change the appearance of a particular pointer, go to *Settings* in the *Start* menu and select *Control Panel*. In the next window, double-click on *Mouse* to see the *Mouse Properties* window. Use the *Pointers* sheet to

select a pointer to change, for example, the *Busy* pointer, then click *Browse....* Select one of the cursors you downloaded from the list in the *Browse* window, and click *OK.* The next time your computer is busy, you'll see an animated alien instead of the hour glass pointer.

Using the **Browse** *window to select a new cursor*

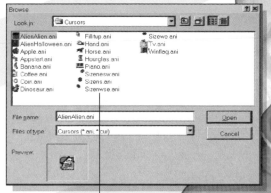

Animated cursor files

Your desktop could be invaded by aliens like these.

You can get close to earthquakes, volcanoes and hurricanes safely by using your computer. The Internet gives you access to pictures and film clips of natural disasters. You can also follow the latest news about events as they happen.

83 EXPLORE AN EARTHQUAKE SITE

In 1995, an earthquake devastated the Japanese city of Kobe. Over 4,000 people were killed, and around 120,000 houses were damaged or destroyed.

To see the chaos caused by the earthquake, go to the Kobe City Web site at **http://www.kobe-cufs.ac.jp/kobe-city/quake/index.html**. Click on the *The Archives of 1995-1996* link to see a list of pictures taken of the city on different dates throughout that year.

Since the disaster, Kobe has gradually been rebuilt. To see how the rebuilding process was progressing two years after the disaster, use your browser's *Back* button to return to the site's home page. Click on *The Archives of 1997* link. On the page which appears, click on *A Pictorial News Brief*. You will see a page with thumbnail images of new and rebuilt buildings.

The Kobe site is regularly updated. You might like to create a short cut to it so you can check up on how rebuilding work is progressing. You can find out how to do this in project 2.

Pictures from the Web which show how Kobe has recovered since the earthquake

(84) TRACK THE PATH OF A HURRICANE

On the Web you can follow the paths of tropical storms and hurricanes. One site which has maps that show the movement of hurricanes is The Hurricane & Storm Tracking Web site at **http://hurricane.terrapin.com/**.

This site uses programs called Java™ applets to show images of moving storms. Java is a programming language which is used to make pictures on Web pages move, or change, when you click on them. To see Java applets, you will need *Netscape Navigator 3.0*, *Internet Explorer 3.0*, or a later version of either browser.

To watch the movement of a storm that took place in 1997, follow the link to *Hurricane Plots and Data 1886-1997*, select *1997* from the drop-down list of years, and click on the name of a storm. A map will download showing where the storm occurred. Click on it to follow the path of the storm.

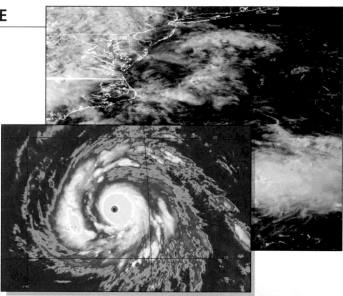

Satellite pictures of tropical storms from the Earth Science Enterprise site at http://www.hq.nasa.gov/office/ese/gallery/

(85) SEE LIVE VOLCANO PICTURES

You can look through devices called Web cameras to watch events as they occur across the world. Web cameras are attached to computers and transmit pictures to Web sites. The pictures are updated at regular intervals.

You can actually use a Web camera to try to see a live volcano. One site where you can do this is at **http://www.actrix.gen.nz/ruapehu/**. It contains pictures taken by a Web camera located near a volcano called Mount Ruapehu in New Zealand.

When Mount Ruapehu is inactive, the camera does not broadcast current pictures. If this is the case, click on the *Best pictures & movies* link to view pictures of the last big eruption. To see a film clip you will need the *Quicktime* plug-in. (For information about downloading plug-ins see project 11.)

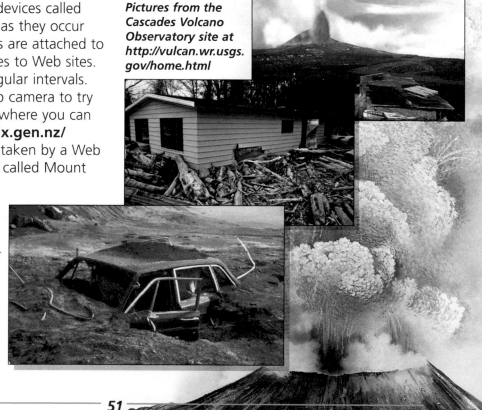

Pictures from the Cascades Volcano Observatory site at http://vulcan.wr.usgs.gov/home.html

Using the Web is a great way to visit museums and galleries all over the world. You can copy famous paintings onto your computer or publish your own works of art.

86 VISIT AN INTERACTIVE EXHIBIT

You can explore the exhibits on display in a museum by visiting its Web site. A good place to try is the Exploratorium site at **http://www.exploratorium.edu/**.

The Exploratorium home page

To see an exhibit, click on *Digital Library* on the home page. From the page which appears, select *Electronic Exhibits*. A list of links will appear. Click on one to download an exhibit.

The exhibit shown below studies how people remember faces. The faces of three famous people have been pasted onto a picture of Elvis.

People visiting the exhibit are asked to guess the identity of these famous faces.

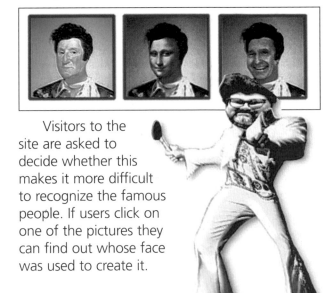

Visitors to the site are asked to decide whether this makes it more difficult to recognize the famous people. If users click on one of the pictures they can find out whose face was used to create it.

A cartoon from the Exploratorium Web site

87 GET SOME ART WALLPAPER

As you explore museums and galleries online, you may come across a picture you particularly like. You could use this to decorate your desktop. A layer of patterns or pictures that covers your desktop is called wallpaper.

To use a picture from the Web as your wallpaper, wait until the picture has completely downloaded, then click on it with your right mouse button. From the menu which appears, select *Set As Wallpaper*. When you close your browser, and any other programs you have open, you will see the picture on your desktop. Depending on how your computer is set up, the picture will either appear in the middle of your desktop, or in a repeated pattern like tiles on a wall.

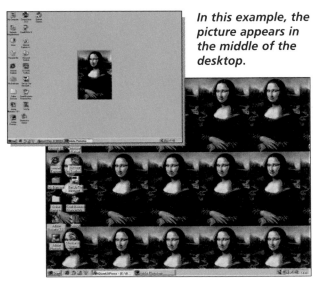

In this example, the picture appears in the middle of the desktop.

In this example, the picture has been tiled.

You can change the way the picture is displayed. To do this in *Windows 95*, go to the *Start* menu and select *Settings*, then *Control Panel*. Double-click on the *Display* icon in the *Control Panel* window. The *Display Properties* dialog box will appear. On the *Background* sheet, select *Center* to see the picture in the middle of the page *or Tile* to see it repeated to cover your desktop. Click *OK* to finish.

88. CREATE AN ART SCRAPBOOK

You could put together your own art scrapbook with material from the Web. This scrapbook will be a computer document containing a selection of pictures and some information about them.

Choose a picture from the Web.

Insert text and pictures from the Web into a word processing program.

You can find suitable material by searching the Web by key word. To find pictures by a particular artist, use the artist's name and the word "painting", for example **+Monet +painting**. When you find a picture you like, save it as in project 19. To find information about a picture you have saved, search the Web using its title. Save the text you find as in project 56.

Once you have gathered some material, go offline. Start a new document in a word processing program such as *Microsoft®Word*. Copy the pieces of text into this document using the method described in project 56. To add a picture select *Insert* and *Object*. In the window that appears, click on *Create from File*, and then *Browse*. Find one of the pictures you saved, and click on *OK*. The picture, or an icon representing it, will appear in your document. To save your scrapbook, select *Save* from the *File* menu.

89. SEND YOUR OWN PICTURES TO A WEB GALLERY

Try getting your artwork displayed at an online art gallery. There are several galleries on the Web which invite anyone to submit their own artwork for display. One such site is the Children's Art Gallery at **http://redfrog. norconnect.no/~cag/**.

For artwork to appear on the Web, it needs to be saved as a computer document. Artwork on paper can be turned into a computer file by a machine called a scanner (see page 7). This process is called scanning in. If you don't have access to a scanner, companies which develop photographs can often scan in pictures for you.

A scanner divides a picture into tiny dots known as pixels or picture elements. It records information about each pixel and stores all the information it collects as a computer file. You use "imaging" software to tell a scanner how many pixels to divide a picture into. The number of pixels in an image is known as its resolution. It is usually measured in dots per inch (dpi).

Art Web sites usually contain clear instructions for submitting pictures. They normally state what resolution your pictures should be. Most pictures on the Web have a resolution of 75 dpi.

When you have scanned in a picture, use the imaging software to save it as a *GIF* or *JPEG* file. These are the file formats most commonly used for Web images.

The Children's Art Gallery displays artwork by people from all over the world.

Using the Internet is a good way of finding out about things to do, planning days out, and discovering what is going on all over the world. Cameras linked to Net computers allow you to look at some of the places you may want to visit.

90) FIND LOCAL LISTINGS

Newspapers, magazines and Web sites often provide information about activities happening in the near future. Events, such as live music, exhibitions and plays, are grouped together in "listings".

You could use a search engine (see project 3) to find a Web site with listings for the city closest to where you live. Use the name of the city and the word **listings** as key words, for example, **+Glasgow +listings**. On the results pages, click on a link to see a listings site.

Cities and towns all over the world have Web sites that publicize local events.

91) PLAN A SUBWAY JOURNEY

You can plan a subway journey in over 50 different cities throughout the world using the Subway navigator Web site at **http://metro.jussieu.fr:10001/**.

A map of the Paris Metro from Subway navigator

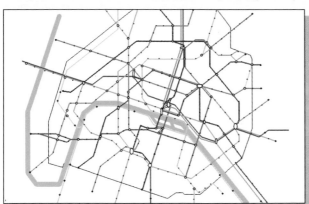

This site helps you to plan a journey between two stations. It tells you the stations your train will stop at and where you need to change trains. For some cities it will even show you your route on a map.

You could, for example, find out how to get from the Gare du Nord station in Paris to Musée du Louvre station, using the Paris Métro. From the Subway navigator home page, click on *Paris*. An online form will appear. Type in **Gare du Nord** next to *Departure station*, and **Musée du Louvre** next to *Arrival station*. Click on *Compute route*. A page will download showing approximately how long the journey will take and the stations you will pass through. To view the route on a map, click on *display*. A map of the Paris Métro will download.

(92) SEE LIFE IN A LOCAL STREET

Some towns have set up Web cameras so that people using the Web can have a bird's eye view of what life is like there. (Find out more about Web cameras in project 85.) Sometimes you can see pictures which were taken just a few seconds ago. You can find sites like this by searching the Web using the phrase **"web camera"**.

The English town of Colchester is one town that has a Web camera. You can see its main street. To see a current picture of the street, go to the Actual Size site at **http://www.actual.co.uk/streetcam.html**. You can use your *Reload* button to update the picture.

The Colchester Web camera site

(93) LOOK AT A MAP SHOWING YOUR STREET

There are very detailed maps of many major cities on the Web. You can use these to help plan a journey or a day out.

A good place to find maps is the Mapquest Web site at **http://www.mapquest.com/**. To download a map showing a particular street click on *Interactive Atlas (Maps)* on the home page. An online form will appear. Type in the name of a street and its location. For streets outside the USA, you will need to click on the *(or, select country from list)* link. Select the country you require from the list which appears. The country's name will appear in the *Country* box on the online form. Click on the *Search* button to finish.

Mapquest can generate local maps for lots of parts of the world.

If Mapquest finds your chosen street, a page will download with one or more small maps. Click on the relevant map to see a larger version.

Maps showing an address in New York

Click on part of the map to enlarge it more.

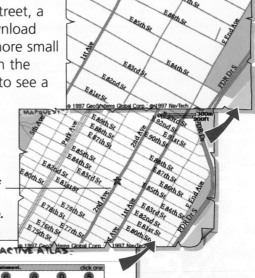

*Select **Recenter Map and Zoom In**, then click on the map to enlarge part of it.*

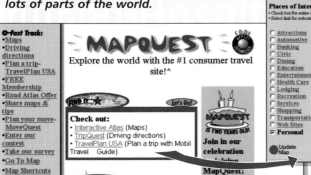

55

It's surprisingly simple to create your own Web pages. There are two methods you can use. You can either add a code called HTML to a text document to turn it into a Web page, or you can use a program called a Web editor.

Projects 96-101 show you how to create a basic Web page with a Web editor called *Microsoft® FrontPage®Express*. This comes with the browser *Microsoft Internet Explorer 4*, which you can download from **http://www. microsoft.com/**. Start by designing a Web page on your computer. There is information about putting your page on the Web on page 59.

Plan what words and pictures you want to put on your Web page on a piece of paper.

94 VISIT SOME PERSONAL WEB SITES

You can get ideas of things to include on your Web page by looking at other people's sites. People create sites about all kinds of subjects ranging from film stars to soccer. One collection of personal sites is GeoCities, at **http://www.geocities.com/**. To find links to personal sites choose a category, such as *Fashion, Sport* or *Games*, on the home page.

All Web pages and sites are stored on computers called host computers so that Net users can see them. GeoCities provides people with space on host computers free of charge.

Most Internet access providers (see page 7) offer a certain amount of free space for their customers' Web pages.

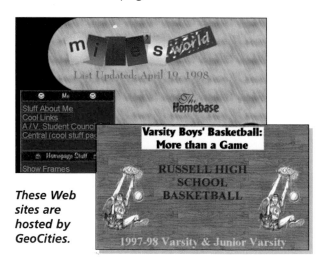

These Web sites are hosted by GeoCities.

95 SET UP A WEB PAGE USING HTML

Try setting up a Web page using HTML. HTML is a set of instructions which tell a browser how to display the information on a Web page. An HTML instruction is called a tag. It appears in brackets like these **< >**.

To set up a very simple page yourself, open a text editing program and create a new document. Type in the codes that appear in brackets exactly as shown below, but you can replace the words outside brackets with your own words. The information that you type in between the two Body tags is the information that will appear on the Web page.

```
<HTML>
<HEAD>
<TITLE>My Page</TITLE>
</HEAD>
<BODY>The text on your page</BODY>
</HTML>
```

Put the title of your page here.

Type in any information you want to include on your Web page here.

Save your page by selecting *Save As* in the *File* menu. Select *Plain text* or *Text document* in the *Save as type* box. Name the file *page.htm*. Save the file into your projects folder (see page 7).

To look at your page, start up your browser. Select *Open, Open File*, or *Open Page* in the *File* menu. Select *page.htm*. Your page will appear. See page 59 for information about transferring a page onto the Web.

(96) USE A WEB EDITOR

Web editors are easier to use than HTML (see project 95). You don't need to know any HTML code to create Web pages with a Web editor.

To create a basic page using *FrontPage Express*, start up the program and type some text into the window. You can then use the buttons on the tool bar to add pictures and links, make text larger or smaller, and alter the background of your page.

FrontPage Express always shows the page you're working on as it will appear when seen through a browser. To save your page, select *Save* in the *File* menu. Name the file *web.htm* and save it into your projects folder, as in project 95.

A Web page in FrontPage Express

The FrontPage Express menu and tool bars

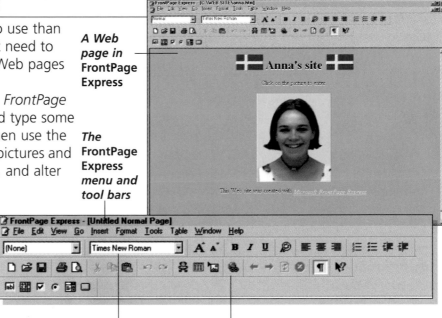

Drop-down list of fonts   **Use this button to insert a picture.**

(97) CHANGE THE TEXT STYLE

The text on a Web page must be easy for people to read. You can use different styles and sizes of text to set out the contents of your page clearly. Web text has seven different sizes. Size 1 is the smallest, and size 7 is the largest.

You can also change the look of your text by making it bold or putting it in italics. To do this, select the text and click on the *Bold*, or the *Italic* button.

Bold

Italic

This writing is **bold.**

This piece of writing is in **italics.**

Use the bold or italic buttons to get these different styles of text.

You can change the "font" you are using for your text. A font is a distinctive style of lettering. Each style has a different name, for example Times Roman and Helvetica. Try out a few to find one you like. To change the font of a piece of text, highlight it and select a font from the drop-down list on the tool bar.

Examples of different fonts

These letters are size 7
This is size 1
This is size 4

You can use these different text sizes on your page.

Enlarge

Reduce

To make a piece of text bigger in *FrontPage Express*, highlight it with your mouse and click once on the *Enlarge* button on the tool bar. This will make it one size larger. To make text smaller, select it and click on the *Reduce* button once.

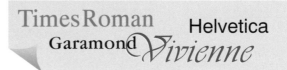

Times Roman   Helvetica
Garamond *Vivienne*

98 CREATE A BACKGROUND

When you create a Web page using *FrontPage Express* (see project 96), it will have a white background. You can make it brighter or more interesting by using a "tiled" background which you create yourself. A tile is a small picture which is repeated to form the background of your page.

Create a tile using a graphics program, for example *Windows 95's Paint*. Open the program and select *Attributes* from the *Image* menu. Specify a canvas size of 3cm by 3cm. Draw an image on your canvas. Keep the image quite pale, so that you will still be able to read the text which will appear on top of the background.

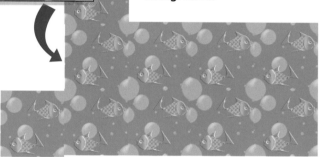

This tile creates a fish background.

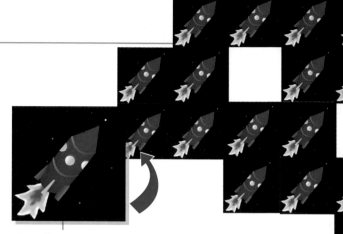

This tile creates a background like this.

To save your tile, select *File* and *Save As*. Give it the name *tile.gif* and save it into your *Projects* folder (see page 7).

To use the tile to create a background on your Web page, start *FrontPage Express*, go to the *Format* menu and select *Background*. The *Page Properties* window will appear. On the *Background* sheet, select the *Background Image* box. Click on *Browse* and the *Select Background Image* window will appear. Find *tile.gif*, highlight it and click on *Open*. Click *OK* in the *Page Properties* window.

You will see your tile repeated to form a background on your page.

99 ADD A PHOTOGRAPH

You can use photographs to decorate your Web pages, or as a way of presenting information. For example, you could add a photograph to your Web page to show a sports team you play for, or a band you belong to. To add a photograph to a Web page, you need to start by saving it on your computer. You will need to convert it into a file your computer can use (see project 89).

In *FrontPage Express*, place your cursor where you want to insert the picture on your Web page. Click on the *Add Image* button. In the *Image* box, click on *Browse*. Find the name of your photograph file, and double-click on it.

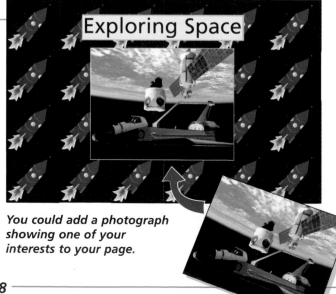

You could add a photograph showing one of your interests to your page.

100 CREATE HYPERLINKS

The links on Web pages are called hyperlinks. You can create hyperlinks to join your Web page to other sites. Visitors to your site can follow hyperlinks to find out more about a subject. For example, if your page includes some information about the pop star Madonna, you could create a link to a site belonging to her record company or a page where you can hear one of her songs.

In *FrontPage Express*, choose a word, phrase, or picture to turn into a link, and highlight it using your mouse. Click on the *Link* tool on your button bar. The *Create Hyperlink* box will appear. In the *URL:* box, type the URL of the page you are linking to. Click on *OK*.

Barbara also has a web page

A hyperlink

The piece of text or picture you choose will be turned into a hyperlink. A text link will turn blue, and it will be underlined. A picture link will not look any different on your screen in *FrontPage Express* but some browsers may place a border around it. You can tell if a picture on a Web page is a hyperlink by passing your mouse over it. If a picture is a hyperlink your mouse pointer will turn into a hand pointer.

101 SAY HELLO TO VISITORS

It's possible to add a sound clip to your Web page so that it plays automatically when someone downloads your page. To record a sound you will need to use a microphone, and a sound recording program such as *Sound Recorder*, which is provided with *Windows 95*.

Say, for example, you want to include a greeting. Start up *Sound Recorder*, click on the *Record* button, and say "hello" into your microphone. Then click on the *Stop* button.

You have now created a sound file. Select *Save As* from the *File* menu to save it, and name it *hello.wav*. Once you've saved your sound file, you can click on the *Play* button to hear it replayed.

The **Sound Recorder** *window*

Play   Stop   Record

To add the sound to your page, go to the *Insert* menu in *FrontPage Express* and select *Background Sound*. Use the *Browse* window to select your sound's filename. Your page won't look any different, but when someone downloads it they will hear you saying hello.

PUTTING YOUR PAGE ON THE WEB

When you have completed your Web page you can put it on the Web. This is called uploading. After you upload your page, anyone surfing the Web will be able to see it.

The exact uploading method will vary depending on who is hosting the page (see project 94). To get full instructions look at your host's Web site, or call their helpline.

The Internet brings the world to your computer. This means that you might come across things you don't like. Follow the guidelines on this page, and throughout the book, to stay safe as you use the Internet.

 A computer virus is a program which attacks your computer's memory and can cause it permanent damage. When using the Net, it's possible to download a computer virus with another program by accident. Use a virus checker program on all the files you download before you open them. You can get an evaluation version of a virus checker from **http://www.drsolomon.com/**. Regularly check your entire C drive for viruses. (Many experts suggest that you should do this once a week.)

 If you receive an e-mail containing anything you don't like, delete it immediately.

 If you find anything on the Web which makes you feel upset or uncomfortable, use your browser's *Stop* button, and visit another page instead.

 Never arrange to meet someone in person whom you've only met on the Internet.

 Don't give your full name, address or telephone number, to someone you have only met on the Net. Remember that the people you meet there are strangers and may not be who they say they are.

USING FILTERS

There are a number of programs which you can install on your computer that will prevent it downloading unpleasant material. These programs are called filters, and they work by blocking access to certain types of material on the Internet. You can download them from their Web sites.

Some of the most popular Web filters and their URLs

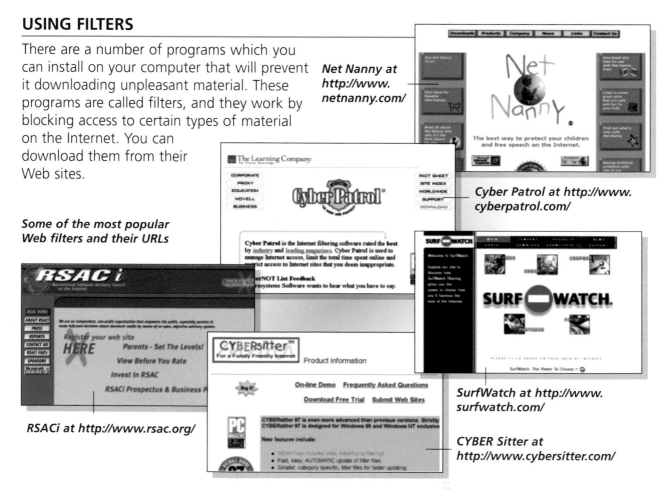

Net Nanny at http://www. netnanny.com/

Cyber Patrol at http://www. cyberpatrol.com/

SurfWatch at http://www. surfwatch.com/

CYBER Sitter at http://www.cybersitter.com/

RSACi at http://www.rsac.org/

Here is a list of Internet words you may come across while you are using this book. Some of these words have more than one meaning. The definitions here are the ones which apply to the Internet. Any word which appears in *italic* type is defined elsewhere in the glossary.

analog signals Waves that can travel along telephone lines.

applet A tiny program written in a programming language called *Java*.

avatar A small, movable picture which represents a computer user in a *virtual world*.

bit The smallest amount of computer data.

bookmark (or short cut). A *browser* option which allows you to *download* a *Web page* without typing its *URL*.

bps (bits per second). The unit used to measure how fast data is transferred between two computers.

browser A piece of *software* which finds and displays *Web pages*.

cache The part of a computer's memory where *Web pages* that have been *downloaded* are stored temporarily.

cyberspace The imaginary space that you travel around when you use the *Net*.

digital signals Electrical pulses produced by a computer.

directory A program which puts *Web pages* into different categories which can be searched.

domain name The part of a *URL* that specifies the kind of organization that owns the *host* computer on which the page or site is stored.

dots per inch (dpi). Measurement of how clear a picture will appear when it has been converted into computer data using a *scanner*.

download To copy files, such as *Web pages* or programs, onto your computer.

eCash (electronic cash, digital cash or online cash). Computer data with the same value as paper and metal money.

e-mail (electronic mail). A way of sending text messages from one computer to another.

encryption Using a complex code to keep information secret.

FAQs (Frequently Asked Questions). The answers to questions most often asked by new *newsgroup* members or visitors to a *Web site*.

freeware *Software* that is free to use.

FTP (File Transfer Protocol). The system used to transfer files between computers over the *Net*.

GIF *Graphics* file format used on the *Web*.

graphics Pictures created using a computer.

hardware The equipment that makes up a computer or a *network*.

home page An introductory page which contains links to other pages on a *Web site*.

host A computer connected to the *Net* which holds information that can be accessed by other Net users.

HTML (HyperText Mark-Up Language). The computer code added to word processed documents to turn them into *Web pages*.

hyperlink (or link). A piece of text or *graphic* which links one *Web page* to another.

hypertext A word or group of words which are *hyperlinks*.

icon A small picture which you can click on to make your computer do something, or which shows that your computer is already doing something.

Internet (or the Net). The worldwide computer *network* which is made up of many smaller networks.

Internet phone A system which lets you make telephone calls via the *Net*.

Internet service providers (ISPs) also known as **Internet access providers** (IAPs). Companies that sell *Net* connections to people.

IRC (Internet Relay Chat). A way of having a conversation with other *Net* users by typing messages and reading their responses.

Java A programming language used to add interactive features to *Web pages*.

JPEG *Graphics* file format used on the *Web*.

key word Any word that you ask a *search engine* to look for.

lurking Reading a *newsgroup* without *posting* any messages to it.

mailbox A place where an *IAP* keeps *e-mail* for a user.

mailing list A discussion group where group members receive messages by *e-mail*.

modem (MOdulate/DEModulate). A device that allows computer data to be sent down an analog telephone line.

moderated A *newsgroup* or *mailing list* in which articles are checked for suitability before they are *posted*.

multimedia A combination of *graphics*, sound and animation.

Netiquette A code of conduct, developed by *Internet* users, which outlines acceptable and unacceptable ways of behaving on the Net.

network A number of computers and other devices that are linked together so that they can share information and equipment.

newsgroup A discussion group where people with the same interests can *post* messages and see other people's responses.

newsreader A program that lets you send and read the messages in *newsgroups*.

off-line Not connected to the *Net*.

online Connected to the *Net*.

online form Item on a *Web page* which you can fill out to send information via the *Web*.

plug-in A piece of *software* you can add to your *browser* to enable it to perform extra functions, such as displaying video clips.

post To place a message in a *newsgroup* so that other members can read it.

Push channel A *browser* window which gathers information while you're online. You can use a channel to get a constant supply of personalized information.

scanner A device used to make a digital copy of a picture so that a computer can read it.

search engine A program which searches for *Web pages* which contain particular words.

secure server A *server* which has safety features to enable information to be sent to it securely.

serial port A socket on a computer through which a *modem* can be connected.

server A computer which connects individual computers to the *Internet*.

shareware *Software* which you can try out before having to pay for it.

software Programs that enable computers to carry out certain tasks.

source code The *HTML* code that makes up a particular *Web page*.

subscribe Add your name to a *mailing list* or *newsgroup*.

tag An *HTML* instruction.

thumbnail A picture shown on a *Web page*, which you can click on to see a larger version.

upload To copy files, via the *Net*, from your computer to another computer.

URL (Uniform Resource Locator or Universal Resource Locator). The specific address of a *Web page*.

videoconferencing Talking to someone via the *Net* so that they can see and hear you.

Virtual Reality (VR). The use of 3-D computer *graphics* to draw places which you can move around.

virtual world A place created by a computer.

virus A program which interrupts the normal functioning of your *hardware* or *software*.

wallpaper The background display on your computer's desktop.

Web camera A camera which puts pictures directly onto the *Net* via a computer.

Web editor A program which lets you create a *Web page* without knowing *HTML* code.

Web page A computer document written in *HTML* and linked to other pages by *hyperlinks*.

Web site A collection of *Web pages* set up by an organization or an individual.

World Wide Web (also known as the Web). A huge collection of information available on the *Internet*. The information is divided up into *Web pages* which are joined together by *hyperlinks*.

zip To make files smaller by compressing them.

ACKNOWLEDGEMENTS

Every effort has been made to trace the copyright holders of the material in this book. If any rights have been omitted, the publishers offer their sincere apologies and will rectify this in any future edition.

Usborne Publishing Ltd. has taken every care to ensure that the instructions contained in this book are accurate and suitable for their intended purpose. However, they are not responsible for the content of, and do not sponsor, any Web site not owned by them, including those listed below, nor are they responsible for any exposure to offensive or inaccurate material which may appear on the Web.

Microsoft®Windows®95, Microsoft® Internet Explorer, Microsoft®Word and Microsoft®FrontPage®Express are either registered trademarks or trademarks of Microsoft Corporation in the United States and other countries. Netscape, Netscape Navigator, and the N logo are registered trademarks of Netscape Communications Corporation in the United States and other countries. Netscape Messenger, Netscape Communicator, Collabra, and Netcaster are also trademarks of Netscape Communications Corporation, which may be registered in other countries. Java and all Java-based trademarks and logos are trademarks or registered trademarks of Sun Microsystems, Inc. in the United States and other countries.

Photographs
Cover Gateway P5-200 Multimedia PC courtesy of Gateway.
Jurgen Klinsmann courtesy of Empics Ltd.
Saturn: Chris Bjornberg/Science Photo Library.
Mona Lisa: SuperStock Ltd (also p.52).
Tutankhamun: SuperStock Ltd.
Starfield: SuperStock Ltd.
Guitar and pasta photos: Howard Allman.
p.2 Optical disk: Telegraph Colour Library (also p.44).
p.3 Biker: Empics (also p.21).
p.5 Videoconferencing images courtesy of Intel®Corp (also p.43).
p.6 Computer courtesy of Apple Computers.
Accura 288 Message Modem supplied by Hayes Microcomputer Products, Inc.
HP Netserver E50 courtesy of Hewlett-Packard Ltd.
Earth from space: European Space Agency/Science Photo Library.
p.7 Microphone courtesy of Creative Labs (also p.42).
HP Deskjet 820CXi printer courtesy of Hewlett-Packard Ltd.
Connectix QuickCam VC used courtesy of Connectix Corporation.
Scanner courtesy of Epson Ltd.
p.18 Dolphin photo: David Hofmann.
p.19 Macaws: Tony Stone Images.
p.20 Tennis Player: SuperStock Ltd (also p.1).

Tennis ball: SuperStock Ltd (also p.1).
Snowboarder: SuperStock Ltd.
American footballer: The Stock Market Photo Agency UK.
pp.22-23 Musical instruments: Howard Allman.
p.25 Hong Kong: The Stock Market Photo Agency UK.
p.34 Statue: The Stock Market Photo Agency UK (also p.1).
Writing montage: SuperStock Ltd (also p.1).
Prayer Book: Tony Stone Images (also p.1).
p.35 Computer: SuperStock Ltd.
Pile of books: The Stock Market Photo Agency UK.
p.39 Food: Howard Allman.
p.42 Speakers courtesy of Creative Labs.
p.44 Money: Telegraph Colour Library.
Gift, t-shirt, flowers: Ray Moller, Amanda Heywood, Sue Atkinson.
p.48 UFO: The Stock Market Photo Agency UK.
p.49 Alien art: Gary Bines.
p.53 Painting: Vanessa Wilson.

Screen shots
Cover Louvre Museum, available in four languages, used with permission.
http://www.louvre.fr
With thanks to NASA.
beeb Sport home page © BBC Worldwide Ltd 1998, photo within page © Allsport 1998.
Beatles page used with permission.
http://home.texoma.net/~a7204/

aaron/beatles
Tour Egypt home page used with permission. **http://www.touregypt.net/**
Cyber Tiger page copyright 1998 National Geographic Society, all rights reserved.
Tiger image from Tammy's Tiger Temple site, used with permission. **http://www.tholyoake.edu/~tlouie/Tiger.htm**
National Pasta Association page used with permission. **http://www.ilovepasta.org/**
p.4 German government site used with permission.
http://www.bundesregierung.de/
p.5 CU-SeeMe trademark and copyright © 1993, 1994, 1995, 1996, 1997, 1998, Cornell University (also p.43). **http://cu-seeme.cornell.edu/**
Avatars courtesy of Onlive, Inc. (also p.43, with screen shot).
p.8 Screen shot reprinted by permission from Microsoft Corporation.
With thanks to the White House.
p.9 AltaVista reproduced with the permission of Digital Equipment Corporation. AltaVista and the AltaVista logo are trademarks of Digital Equipment Corporation (also pages 11 and 47).
Excite, WebCrawler, the Excite logo and the Webcrawler logo are trademarks of Excite, Inc. and may be registered in various jurisdictions. Excite screen display copyright 1995-1997 Excite, Inc.
Hotbot copyright © 1994-97 HotWired, Inc. All rights reserved.
Infoseek logo reprinted by permission. Infoseek and the Infoseek logo are

First published in 1998 by Usborne Publishing, Ltd, Usborne House, 83-85 Saffron Hill, London EC1N 8RT, England. www.usborne.com Copyright © 1998 Usborne Publishing Ltd. The name Usborne and the device ⊖ are Trade Marks of Usborne Publishing Ltd. *All rights reserved.* No part of this publication may be reproduced, stored in a retrieval system or transmitted in any form or by any means, electronic, mechanical, photocopying, recording or otherwise, without the prior permission of the publisher. UE.
First published in America in 1999.
Printed in Spain.